Animal Stories and Poems for Children

By
Edward A. Salerno

E-BookTime, LLC
Montgomery, Alabama

Animal Stories and Poems for Children

Copyright © 2007 by Edward A. Salerno

ISBN: 978-1-59824-705-3

First Edition
Published October 2007
E-BookTime, LLC
6598 Pumpkin Road
Montgomery, AL 36108
www.e-booktime.com

DEDICATION

This book is dedicated to Steven, my fine son, who allowed me to read to him for many hours and who read to me (Charlie Brown, the comics, etc.) for many hours and who has given me many, many happy memories.

With remembrance to Mom and Dad!

A PRAYER:

Give parents the grace and wisdom to treat their children with love and kindness.

Give single people the grace and wisdom to stop bringing children into the world who will be neglected and abandoned.

Contents

Poetry

GREETINGS

Hello, all my little friends,
I hope your day was bright.
I am so very happy
As I visit you tonight,
Coming into every home
To tell you special stories,
To tell you special poems.

I speak to every little ear
These words for only you to hear
So now it's time, I shall begin.
I hope that you're all snuggled in
To hear the stories, some in rhyme,
And hope you'll have a happy time.

Mr. Ed

DEXTER THE DEER

Dexter lived deep in the forest. Now that he was one year old, he was considered an adult and he had to leave his mother. He was sorry to leave but all male deer had to leave their mothers when they became one year old. It was time for them to take care of themselves. So Dexter licked his mother's cheek and said good-bye. She smiled bravely and said, "Just remember all that I taught you and you will be fine." This was not the first child she had to part with.

But Dexter did not feel like an adult. He was small for his age and his antlers were not as big as the other deer his age. He would rather have stayed with his mother at least for a little while longer. But she could not let him.

Then Dexter saw his friend Buck and his spirits picked up. Dexter liked Buck because he was nice and he was also small, like Dexter. The other male deer used to tease Dexter and Buck because they were small. So Buck and Dexter used to play with the smaller animals - the rabbits, squirrels, possums and chipmunks.

Dexter rushed over. Buck was glad to see Dexter. He didn't like leaving his mother either. "Hi, Buck," Dexter called.

"Hi, Dexter," Buck replied. "I was just going over to a swell clover field and have something to eat. Want to come?"

"Sure," replied Dexter.

As they walked along, they talked about how sad they felt about leaving their mothers. "But all males do it and look how happy our fathers are," Buck exclaimed.

Dexter felt better. "Yes, you are right."

"Come on," Buck shouted. "I'll race you to the clover field." And he was off.

Dexter took right after him. Soon they arrived breathless at a nice field thick with clover. They began chomping immediately. After several minutes, they were full.

"Let's rest a while and then go down to the creek for a cool drink," Buck said.

"OK," Dexter agreed. The two stretched out in the lush clover.

"Boy," said Buck. "This is swell. I like it already."

"Me, too," answered Dexter but not with as much enthusiasm as his friend.

They were quiet for a moment. Then Buck began to sniff the air. Dexter raised his head and sniffed, too.

"What's that smell?" Buck asked.

"I don't know. It sure is strange."

The two stood up and sniffed in all directions. Suddenly Dexter's mother rushed up.

"There's a fire. Quick, run! Go to the lake. It is safe there." Then she was gone.

Buck and Dexter saw a little fire once but the older deer quickly stamped it out. "Fires are very dangerous in the forest," they were told.

As they were about to flee, Dexter suddenly remembered, "What about our little friends?" he asked. "Maybe they cannot run fast enough to get to the lake."

"You are right," said Buck. "Let's go and help them."

So the two young deer hurried through the forest calling for their friends.

"Come on, jump on our backs," Dexter shouted.

All of the smaller animals climbed up on the backs of Dexter and Buck and clung to their fur. The mother possums and their babies hung by their tails from the deer's antlers. They looked like funny ornaments.

"Is everybody here?" Buck asked.

"Yes," all the mothers answered.

As soon as all the animals were safely on board, Dexter shouted, "Hang on tight!"

Then Dexter and Buck headed for the lake as fast as their legs could carry them. They raced through the bushes and jumped over fallen trees. The smell was much stronger and the forest had become very warm. They could hear the crackle of the flames as they rapidly consumed trees, bushes and dry grass. The fire was right behind them.

They arrived at the lake, panting for air and exhausted. All the little animals jumped off and hovered close to the shore. Most of the other animals were already there and some of the larger animals, like the elk and moose, even stood in the shallow water. All looked towards the glowing sky and the black smoke which billowed over the treetops.

Dexter and Buck found their mothers and went to them. They were all glad to see each other safe. There was much nuzzling and licking.

Then Rory Rabbit hopped over and said, "Dexter and Buck saved our lives. They carried us here on their backs."

All the other animals looked at Dexter and Buck with admiration. Some of the other male deer who used to tease Dexter and Buck were a little embarrassed for not thinking of the little animals. They lowered their heads a little.

"Hooray for Dexter and Buck," Martha Moose called.

Then everyone shouted a big "HOORAY!"

Dexter and Buck felt a little shy but also very proud. Then Dexter's mother whispered to her son, "Being small doesn't mean you can't be brave."

Dexter looked up at his mother and smiled.

Eventually, the fire died out but everything was charred and black. It looked very desolate. Their homes were all destroyed.

Then the king of the deer spoke, "The fire does not permanently destroy the forest. By Spring, new shoots will sprout and new trees will grow. In a few years, the forest will be thicker and greener than ever."

Everyone felt relieved. The king had been through a fire before. He knew what he was talking about.

"We must live in another part of the forest for now," the king continued. "Leave this part to renew itself."

Then they all followed the king who would lead them to their new homes. Dexter and Buck pranced about, imitating the king and giggling. Their mothers couldn't help but smile at the antics of their two adult children.

THE END

JUMBO, THE FASTEST ELEPHANT IN THE JUNGLE

Did you know that long ago in a land very far away lived an elephant, Jumbo was his name?

Although Jumbo weighed 300 pounds, he was only two years old and was still considered a baby. He still drank milk from his mother twice a day so his bones would be very strong and he still liked being close to his mother. So you see he was still a baby.

But Jumbo also liked playing with the other animals in the jungle, too. So when he asked his mom if he could join his friends, she always said, "Yes!" Then he would trumpet and run off to be with his waiting friends.

The only thing that made Jumbo sad was when the animals played chase. No one wanted Jumbo on their side.

"You are too big and too slow!" the lion cub said.

"Yes," said the hyena pup, "Elephants are too big and too slow!"

Then they would all run off, chasing each other all over the jungle, laughing and being noisy, like all children. Jumbo just sat and watched and tried not to cry. He wished he wasn't an elephant, then he could play chase. Sometimes he would even feel very angry about being an elephant.

One day while his friends were playing chase, Jumbo decided not to watch, so he took a walk. That was something his mother warned him not to do. "Never walk off into the jungle by yourself," she told him. And Jumbo promised not to.

But today he was feeling disobedient so he just walked away. And after he had walked a good distance, he heard a loud roar!

That sounds like a lion, Jumbo thought. So he decided to see where this roaring was coming from. Then he heard another roar. "There it is again," he said. This time it was closer so he kept walking.

The next roar was very close but Jumbo could not see any lion. Slowly he moved closer, in the direction of the roar. Then there was another very loud roar, even louder! It came from the tall grass right in front of Jumbo.

"Who's there?" called Jumbo in a timid voice.

"It's me, Leopold," a voice replied.

Leopold was the bravest lion in the jungle and his son, Lonigan, was Jumbo's good friend.

Cautiously he moved forward and then right before him, hidden in some tall grass, was a deep hole and Leopold was at the bottom. It was one of those traps that Jumbo's mother warned him about. The hunters must be in the jungle again.

"I can't get out," roared Leopold. "It is too deep. Hurry and get help before the hunters return."

"I will," called Jumbo, as he peered down at the helpless lion. Then he turned and ran right back to his mother.

As he ran, Jumbo trumpeted loudly for all the animals to hear. And they came together to see what the commotion was all about.

Jumbo's mom knew her son's trumpet and came running. By the time Jumbo reached everyone, they were all in a group.

Jumbo quickly told about poor Leopold being trapped in a hole and that the hunters were coming to get him.

"Oh, dear," cried Jumbo's mom.

"My father," cried Lonigan. "Where is he? I must go to him!"

"Yes," everyone responded, "we must help Leopold!"

"I will show you," called Jumbo. "Follow me!" Then he turned and ran off.

All the other animals were right on his heels. At least for a while! Then Jumbo heard Lonigan call, "Hey, Jumbo, slow down, we can't keep up!"

"Yes," puffed Jumbo's mom, "you are running too fast!"

Jumbo couldn't believe his large ears! He was always told he was too big and too slow so he just believed it! Then he stopped and looked back. Sure enough, he was way ahead of all the other animals. And as soon as they started to catch up, he spun around and ran off.

Now he could hear Leopold roaring for help. They were getting close.

Jumbo got to the hole first and said, "I'm back and I've brought help!"

Leopold looked up but all he could see was Jumbo's eyes staring down at him. Where was the help, he wondered? Then he heard the thundering steps and he knew Jumbo had saved him.

All of the animals stopped at the edge of the hole and stared down. How were they going to get Leopold out?

"I will jump down and boost him up," cried Lonigan.

"He is too big for you to lift and then how will we get you out?" asked Jumbo's mom.

Lonigan lowered his head and began to cry.

"Wait!" said Jumbo's mom. "I have an idea!"

Then she carefully got down on her two front knees, right at the edge of the hole, and lowered her long trunk. "Grab my trunk and I will pull you up!" she instructed.

Leopold wrapped his front and back legs around the thick trunk, making sure his sharp claws did not come out. When he had a good hold, Jumbo's mom slowly rose to her feet, pulling Leopold right out of that hole!

As soon as Leopold was freed from his terrible ordeal, Lonigan climbed right up on his father's back and snuggled in his long, soft mane. He was very happy to have his father safe.

Leopold thanked Jumbo and his mom and everyone who came to help. Then he gave a mighty roar and dashed off to guard his pride's territory. Everyone cheered.

Lonigan said, "Jumbo, you and your mom saved my father. From now on you will always be on my side when we play chase!"

Jumbo couldn't believe his ears. He was so proud and shy that he leaned

14

against his mom who cuddled him with her trunk.

Then Lonigan yelled, "Let's play chase! Come on, Jumbo!"

And all the young animals ran off to play in the jungle. And they were all best friends for the rest of their lives. Jumbo's mom proudly watched her son run off with his friends.

THE END

SPARKY

Sparky stamped impatiently in his stall and swished away pesky flies with his tail. "I wish the children would come," he muttered. "I hope they bring me a carrot and an apple." His mouth watered at the thought of delicious things to eat. He was tired of the dried, old hay he had been munching on all day.

Meanwhile, not far away, the school bell rang and the children in all the classes jumped up excitedly and hurried out of their classrooms. Today was the last day of class - school was out for the summer. The teachers smiled at the enthusiasm of the children and watched their noisy departure.

Leo was glad his seventh grade term was over. As soon as he was outside the building, he looked about for his sister, Ginger. When he didn't see her, he turned to watch the rest of the students filing through the door and shouting excitedly. Leo exchanged greetings with some of his schoolmates.

Then he saw Ginger hurrying through the door. She was always one of the last to get out.

"Hi, Ginger!" Leo called.

Ginger spied her brother and ran to him. "Sorry I'm late," she said. "I had to say good-bye to Ms. Carrol. She's not coming back next year."

Leo grunted and the two walked along side by side to the bus. "Aren't you glad school is over?" Ginger asked. "We are going to have a wonderful summer," she added.

"Yes," answered Leo. "I am looking forward to spending two weeks with grandma and grandpa."

"Me, too," agreed Ginger. "It's always fun to visit them and see the big city."

"Let's take a ride on Sparky before dinner," Leo suggested.

"Oh, yes. We'll have plenty of time to get back and help mom with dinner."

They boarded the bus and soon were on their way.

Leo and Ginger Hubbel lived in the country. Their parents had a little farm where they grew corn and some vegetables. They loved the country and they loved their pets, Sparky and their Collie, Rufus.

They burst through the door to their house with a great commotion. Rufus' barks added to the din. "Land sakes!" cried their mother, "can't you two ever come into the house quietly?"

"No!" they shouted and laughed at their daring.

Mrs. Hubbel smiled at their antics. She knew they were all wound up with school over for the summer.

"Mom," called Ginger, "can we go for a ride on Sparky? We will be back in time to help with dinner."

"Alright," Mrs. Hubbel answered. "Ride out and remind your dad that we are eating earlier tonight."

"Why are we eating earlier?" Leo asked.

Mrs. Hubbel smiled. "That's a surprise. Now change your clothes and run along. Sparky is probably dying to get out of his stall."

The children ran to their rooms. There was a race to see who could get changed faster. There was always a race with those two, Mrs. Hubbel thought.

Soon the doors to their rooms burst opened and they raced out, bumping and jostling each other as they headed for the kitchen. In their hurry to be first, neither tucked their T-shirts into their jeans.

"I beat you!" Leo shouted.

"Did not," Ginger countered.

They went straight to the refrigerator and opened the door. "You take a carrot and I will take an apple," Ginger called.

"No, you take the carrot and I'll take an apple," Leo ordered.

"In a minute, neither of you will take anything," Mrs. Hubbel threatened.

With that, Ginger grabbed an apple and ran to the back door. Leo took a carrot and chased after her. "Not fair! Not fair!" he called. Ginger laughed and was out of the door, with Leo close behind. Rufus ran out right behind Leo and was soon ahead of both of them.

By the time they got to the barn door, they were almost neck and neck, laughing and shouting at each other. As soon as Sparky heard them, he began to nicker. The children stopped at the barn door and quietly opened it. Sparky had his head sticking out of his stall door, with his neck craned as far as he could. His eyes were open wide and his ears were erect. He stomped nervously.

"Sparrrkyy," Leo and Ginger called softly.

Sparky snorted and shook his head. Then he stood very still, looking right at them. "Would you like a treat?" they teased, hiding the apple and carrot behind their backs.

Sparky snorted again as the children slowly advanced. He looked from one to the other, trying to see what they had brought for him.

Keeping their treats out of sight, the children began petting Sparky and talking softly to him. He was impatient for something good to eat and tried to reach behind them. He knew they were hiding something from him.

"OK," Ginger cried. "Here you are." And she produced the apple which Sparky quickly snatched from her extended palm. He chomped noisily on his treat and soon swallowed it. Then he turned to Leo.

"What?" asked Leo. "I don't have anything," he said innocently.

Sparky would have none of that and he bumped Leo with his head. Leo almost lost his balance and he and Ginger laughed at the pony's aggression.

"OK! OK!" Leo cried. He held out the carrot and Sparky quickly bit off half of it. Leo held on to the other half. When Sparky gulped down his first bite, he took the other half from Leo's outstretched hand. The children laughed and petted him for a moment. Then Leo took the bridle from its peg on the wall and put it on the waiting pony.

When he was bridled, Ginger opened the stall door and Sparky trotted out, eager to go for a run. Once outside, Leo jumped on Sparky's back and Ginger climbed on behind. Leo held the rein firmly and called, "All ready?"

"Ready!" answered Ginger and off they galloped, with Rufus racing along.

"Dad's probably checking the corn," Ginger called to her brother.

"Yes. I hope we have a good crop this year. Last year's wasn't too good."

"I know," Ginger replied. Soon they saw their father, bending over, inspecting the young plants. They stopped at the edge of the field, jumped off Sparky and ran to him.

"Hi, Dad!" they called. But this time Rufus was the fastest and he raced between two neatly planted rows, right up to Mr. Hubbel, wagging his tail and woofing.

Mr. Hubbel straightened and turned to greet his visitors. "Well, hello," he smiled. "All through with school?"

"You bet," they answered. "Mom says don't forget to come home early."

"How does the crop look, Dad?" Leo asked.

"So far so good but it's only June. We have a way to go before we can really tell."

He patted his children on the tops of their heads. They pressed against him. "We'll be here to help you all summer, Dad," Ginger assured.

"I know. And you are both a big help. Where are you off to?"

"No place. Just taking a ride before dinner," Leo replied.

"Well, ride along the west fence and see if it needs any fixing. Might as well do that before the corn gets going."

"OK, Dad," the children answered. They turned and started running toward Sparky who was chomping on grass and weeds. Rufus ran past both of them and raced around the pony. Sparky wasn't going to stop eating just because of Rufus so he ignored his antics. When the children were safely mounted, Leo pointed Sparky toward the west fence and they were off in a gallop.

"Hi Ho, Silver!" the children shouted.

They slowed Sparky to a walk and covered the whole western fence line, observing any damage as they rode. There was actually very little of the fence that needed mending but the children took their inspection very seriously. Rufus went this way and that, sniffing the ground as he trotted along.

Suddenly Rufus stopped and looked intently into the tall grass. "Maybe he smells a skunk," Ginger said.

"Oh, no, not that again," Leo exclaimed. "Remember the last time he chased a skunk? PU!"

"PU!" Ginger responded. "Rufus, come!" she ordered. But Rufus was frozen in his tracks, his hind leg quivered with anticipation.

"Rufus!" Leo called. Suddenly, the tall grass rustled. The children stared, trying to see what was hidden. Rufus lowered his head and woofed.

Something was coming through the bushes. Leo and Ginger became nervous. Leo wondered if he should turn Sparky and take off. Then they heard a cry. It sounded human. Suddenly a small child staggered out of the bushes. He cried softly and stared at the children on their pony.

"Why that's little Robbie Lowe," Leo said. "What's he doing out here by himself?"

"Robbie," Ginger called. The little four-year-old tottered towards them, holding out his arms and crying more loudly.

Ginger jumped off Sparky and ran to pick up the little boy. "Oh, it's alright, Robbie," she soothed as she hugged him tightly. "He must have wandered off," she said, looking up at Leo. "Let's take him to dad."

"OK. Hand him to me while you climb up."

Little Robbie didn't like being passed about and he clung tightly to Ginger's neck. She pried him loose and handed the squirming, crying child to Leo. Once seated, she squeezed the boy between her and her brother and Leo set Sparky off at a trot. But the bouncing was too frightening for poor Robbie so Leo slowed Sparky to a walk. Soon the boy quieted and was content to be safely pressed between two warm bodies. In a few minutes Leo and Ginger were calling to their dad.

When Mr. Hubbel saw the child, he hurried over. "We found him by the fence, Dad," Leo said.

"Is he OK?"

"I think so," Ginger replied. Mr. Hubbel gave Robbie a quick inspection. Robbie stared at the stranger but said nothing.

"Take him to the house. Your mother can call the Lowes and see what's going on. He may have just wandered off."

"OK," the children answered and headed toward the house.

As they approached the house, Leo and Ginger called loudly to their mother. Leo swung his foot over Sparky's neck and jumped down. By the time he helped Ginger and Robbie down, Mrs. Hubbel was on the porch. When she saw Robbie she hurried over and took him. Robbie began to cry again.

"What in the world!" Mrs. Hubbel cried.

"We found him by the west fence," Ginger said.

"My gracious, he must have just walked away. Poor Mrs. Lowe must be frantic."

Mrs. Hubbel hurried into the house with Robbie in her arms. She dialed the Lowes.

"Anita, we have Robbie! The children found him wandering by our west fence. . . . . . Oh, yes, he is fine. . . . . OK, we'll be here. Take your time." She hung up the phone.

"The poor woman. She was hysterical. She phoned the sheriff. She's coming right over.

"Now you little dickens," Mrs. Hubbel said, holding Robbie over her head. "What do you mean scaring your poor parents half to death?" Robbie laughed. He recognized Mrs. Hubbel. "Would you like a nice drink of orange juice?"

"Yes, gimme juice, please," the boy replied. Mrs. Hubbel laughed. He was oblivious to all the trouble he caused.

19

Mrs. Hubbel sat the child at the table and poured him a glass of juice. Robbie drank eagerly then called, "More juice, please."

"We were inspecting the west fence," Ginger told her mother.

"And Rufus could tell something was in the bushes so he just froze," added Leo.

"We thought it was a skunk. Then out came Robbie, crying a little bit but not bad," Ginger finished.

"My goodness, I hate to think of what might have happened if you hadn't found him!" Mrs. Hubbel exclaimed.

"It was really Rufus who found him, mom," Leo said. "Yes, Rufus was the one," Ginger added.

Mrs. Hubbel turned to Rufus and said, "Did you do that, you good dog?"

Rufus responded by approaching her with a woof and a wag of his tail. He raised his head to be petted. Mrs. Hubbel caressed his soft fur. The look in his eyes showed his affection as he shifted his weight from one front paw to the other.

In no time a car pulled up to the back of the house. Mrs. Hubbel scooped up Robbie and carried him to the kitchen door. Mr. and Mrs. Lowe hurried up the three steps and across the porch.

"Robbie," Mrs. Lowe called, her arms outstretched. She pulled the boy into her arms and hugged him tightly. Tears streamed down her cheeks. Robbie put his arms around his mother's neck and squeezed. He had an impish smile on his little face.

"I can't explain it," she began. "I just turned my back for a minute and he was gone. He was playing right in the yard."

"The first thing I thought of was the pond. I called Bill and we went there. We searched and yelled. Then Bill ran back to the house and called the sheriff." Then she burst into tears. Bill had one arm around his wife and one around Robbie.

"How did you find him?" Mrs. Lowe asked, after she composed herself.

"We were riding the west fence and Rufus spotted something," Leo said.

"He just froze like there was a bird or some animal in the bushes," Ginger continued. "And then out came Robbie."

"He wasn't really scared or nothing," Leo commented.

"Well, he was crying a little," Ginger countered.

Leo sneered at his sister for not agreeing with him.

"Then we picked him up and brought him home."

"I gave him two glasses of orange juice," Mrs. Hubbel said.

"Well, we will take him home and give him his supper," Mrs. Lowe said. "And you, young man, don't you ever go out of the yard by yourself again. Do you hear me?"

"Yes," Robbie replied shyly and hid his face in his mother's neck.

Everyone laughed. Just then Mr. Hubbel came in.

"Did this little boy get out of the pen?" he teased. Robbie hid his face in his mother's shoulder.

"Yes, he did," she answered and gave the boy a pat on his seat. "He will never, never do that again."

After a little while, the Lowes left and everyone gave a sigh of relief. There could have been a tragedy but it all turned out alright.

"Now let's get cleaned up," Mrs. Hubbel announced.

"We'll help with dinner, mom," Ginger offered.

"No, dear. The surprise is that we are going to town and have pizza and go to the movies. School is over and we are going to celebrate."

Leo and Ginger looked at each other with glee. "Oh, boy, mom, that's swell," Leo replied.

"Yeah, mom and dad, thanks," added Ginger. "This really is a surprise. Do we have to change clothes?"

"No, just wash up. Dad, you'd better change."

"I'll get my best suit and be right with you." Everyone laughed. "Put Sparky in the barn and I'll be out in a minute."

Sparky was waiting patiently where the children left him. Leo and Ginger lead him back to his stall and took off his bridle.

"You got a short ride today, boy," Ginger said to Sparky as she patted his forehead.

"Tomorrow we will give you a good grooming and take you for a long ride," Leo added.

Then they put some fresh hay in his feeder, gave him a pat and left.

Sparky snorted, almost as if he understood. Leo and Ginger laughed.

"Hey," Leo scolded, "You're not Mr. Ed. Don't pretend you understand what we are talking about."

"Oh, Sparky, you are smarter than Mr. Ed or Trigger," Ginger said.

By the time they washed, their parents were ready to go. Leo and Ginger climbed into the back seat of the car and soon they were on the highway, heading for town.

"I want sausage on my pizza," Ginger declared.

"I want mushrooms on mine," Leo said.

Ginger was about to reply when their dad said in a firm tone, "Then we will get a family-sized pizza with mushrooms and sausage."

"And peppers," added mom.

Leo and Ginger looked at each other and giggled. The discussion was over.

Leo leaned over to his sister and whispered, "And tomorrow I give Sparky the apple."

Ginger gave him her famous wait-and-see expression and Leo gave her a poke in her ribs with his elbow. They started giggling again.

"Will you two ever stop?" their mother asked with a sigh.

THE END

21

THE BEAVERS BUILD A DAM

Billy Beaver and Bobby Beaver were swimming in the creek. They had swum and paddled for quite some distance from their previous home which was on a large pond. One day they decided to look for a new home so off they went, down streams and creeks. They decided to take a rest on the bank of this nice creek which wound its way through a lovely forest.

As they rested and chatted about their journey, Casper the cat fish raised his head out of the water.

"Meow!" cried Casper. "How are you today?"

"Hello yourself," replied Billy and Bobby. "We are fine, thank you!"

"Where are you going?" asked Casper.

"We are going to build a new home somewhere," answered Billy.

"Yes, we got tired of our old home," added Bobby.

"Oh, are you thinking of building your home here?" asked Casper.

"Well, we haven't decided," replied Billy.

"This is a nice place," added Bobby.

"Oh, I wish you would build a strong dam here and make a nice lake," Casper said.

"Why would you like us to build here?" asked Billy.

"Because I am the only fish who lives here and if there was a nice lake, lots of fish would live in it and I would have lots of friends to play with. I am very lonely."

"Why don't you swim to a lake where there will be other fish?" asked Bobby.

"I was born here and I love this forest. I want to stay here but sometimes when it rains, the creek swells up and I am carried downstream. Then I have to swim very hard to come back here. If there was a lake, I would not get swept away. It is getting harder and harder for me to swim back. I am afraid that one day I will not have the strength to swim back."

Billy and Bobby waddled off a little distance and entered into a serious discussion. Then they returned, "OK, we have decided to make our new home here. We will build a strong dam first and stop the water from flowing so fast. Then we will build a nice home in the middle of the lake that will be formed by the dam."

"Oh, thank you!" cried Casper. "That will be wonderful. I will love watching you work."

With that, Billy and Bobby began gnawing some strong trees with their sharp teeth. When the trees fell, the two beavers gnawed them to just the right size, dragged them into the creek and positioned them in such a way as to make a dam. Casper watched with great anticipation and awe at how crafty the beavers were. In no time, the trees had dammed the creek and a pond began to form.

Then Billy and Bobby began to gnaw more trees and set about building a home right in the middle of the pond. Part of the beaver's home is under water and part sticks up above the water. So the beavers have no trouble finding their home.

As Billy and Bobby worked on their home, the pond slowly grew larger and larger. Soon there will be a fine lake here, Casper said to himself. He was delighted at the thought and made little leaps out of the water.

Billy and Bobby paid no attention to Casper's antics. They were too busy to take notice. From time to time they stopped working to discuss the construction of their new home. Then it was right back to work. By the next day, Billy and Bobby finished their new home. Then it began to rain. Just a little at first but then harder and harder. The more rain that came down, the larger the pond became. Billy and Bobby checked their dam and made reinforcements where necessary. The dam was holding and the pond was quickly becoming a fine lake.

Casper was overjoyed. He swam about as fast as he could and leaped out of the water from time to time, just like a porpoise. "Hooray! Hooray!" he shouted. Billy and Bobby smiled at the enthusiasm of their new friend. It was a good feeling knowing that they had made this little fish happy.

And before you knew it, a carp appeared in the lake. Casper swam right up to her and gave her a warm greeting.

"Hello!" called Casper. "My name is Casper. Welcome to our new lake."

"Thank you," said the carp. "My name is Clara. I was being carried along by the current of the creek and am most thankful to find this nice lake. I was going so fast that I was afraid my fins were going to be hurt."

"Yes, I had that problem, too but then Billy and Bobby Beaver came and made a dam and built a new home. Now we have this wonderful lake."

"My, this is a nice forest," observed Clara. "The last lake I lived in was not as nice as this. I think I will like living here. Are there any other fish living here?"

"Not yet," replied Casper, "but I bet there will be soon."

Clara smiled. And sure enough, soon there were several other fish swimming around in the lake. They quickly introduced themselves to each other and made friends.

Then one morning, a family of campers came along. There was a man and his wife and their three children.

"This looks like a lovely place," said the lady.

"Yes, it does," agreed her husband.

"Yes! Yes!" cried the children. "Let's stay here."

Soon a tent was erected and a fire started. Billy and Bobby and the fish watched.

"I hope they don't start fishing," worried Clara.

"If they do, don't bite their hook," cautioned Casper.

"No, don't bite the hook," the other fish echoed.

But the campers were not fishing people. They had canned goods, eggs, bacon, vegetables, juice and plenty of water. They talked, sang and laughed and had a swell time together. The next day they all went swimming in the lake.

After a few days, the family packed up their gear, making sure they did not leave any litter, and began to hike. The fish all raised their heads above the water and waved good-bye. The family waved good-bye and soon disappeared along the creek.

"It was swell having campers," said Casper.

"I agree," said Clara. "Maybe we will have lots of nice visitors."

"I hope so," said the other fish.

And so the fish lived happily ever after in the nice lake that Billy and Bobby had created with their dam. And many campers came and enjoyed the lake also.

THE END

HUGH THE GNU

Hugh was a young Gnu who lived on the Great Plains of Africa. He loved to frisk and romp with the other Gnus his age. His mother let him have fun but always kept a watchful eye on him. She never knew when a lion was about and lions loved to catch young Gnus.

The Gnus were a very large herd that roamed vast distances of Africa. They constantly moved along in their search for new grass to feast on. As they grazed, the lions frequently prowled the outskirts of the herd, looking for a sick or injured Gnu, one that would be easy to catch.

Hugh's mother warned him about lions and told him to run away if he ever saw one. "I will, Mother," Hugh promised and then he would turn and scamper away, laughing and calling to his friends. For the most part, the older Gnus paid little heed to the youngsters. They were busy feasting on the long, fresh grass that covered the plain. But they were always on the alert for lions who might be close by.

Hugh saw the lions catch some Gnus so he understood his mother when she warned him to watch out. It frightened him when the herd ran from the lions. Hugh would quickly find his mother and they would race away with all the other Gnus. When the chase was over, all the Gnus settled down to their grazing.

Hugh always stayed close to his mother for a while after a chase. She would nuzzle him and make him feel safe. Then it was off for a run with his friends and everything was back to normal.

Hugh noticed some strange creatures sitting in a strange thing. "Mother, what are those?" he asked.

She smiled and answered, "Those are humans. That thing carries them over the plain just like the monkeys carry their babies on their backs sometimes."

"Oh!" answered Hugh. "Are they dangerous like the lions?"

"No," she answered. "They don't bother us. They seem to like watching the animals."

One day Hugh was racing around with his friends when he tripped and fell with a thud. His mother saw him fall and hurried over. Hugh was a little stunned. He shook his head and then slowly rose to his feet. His mother looked on anxiously.

"Are you all right, dear?" she asked.

Hugh looked about and saw all of his friends staring at him. Even the humans were watching. "I am fine, mother," he answered bravely.

But when he started to run, his ankle hurt very much and he had to stop. He could barely walk. Hugh's mother became very worried. "Stay close to me until your foot is better," she instructed.

Hugh was confused. He could always run. Why was it so hard to walk, he wondered. He hobbled after his mother, feeling pain and embarrassment.

The herd suddenly became nervous. The signals were being given. Lions were about. Hugh could tell his mother was very anxious. She tried to lead him into the center of the herd but it was hard for him to keep up. He limped after her and she moved as slowly as she could, knowing the lions were looking for injured Gnus.

Suddenly the herd panicked and began racing across the grass. Hugh's mother bolted with the rest and Hugh followed but he could only hobble and was soon left behind.

All he could think of was the lions. He knew they always went after the injured ones. Would they catch him, he wondered? "Mother, Mother," he called as he limped along. His foot hurt so badly now.

What would it be like to be caught by a lion? He couldn't imagine. He just kept going but all the Gnus were racing by. Soon he would be left behind. Then he felt a sharp pain in his hind leg. "Ouch!" he gasped. His legs were still moving but he seemed to be getting numb all over. His legs were churning rapidly but he was barely moving. Then slowly, slowly, he lost consciousness and slumped to the ground. The last thing he remembered was seeing the herd running away and a great cloud of dust. "Mother," he whispered. Then nothing!

Slowly Hugh regained consciousness. First he opened his eyes and he could see. Then feelings slowly returned to his body. He tried to get up but he couldn't. He was held down by something. He raised his head and looked about. He was lying on a table. His foot was all wrapped in some white stuff. He thrashed about but was tightly bound.

"There, there, little fellow. It's alright." Then Hugh saw the humans. They petted him gently and soothed him. But his instincts told him to run and he renewed his efforts to get up.

"Better give him a shot," Dr. Jim said.

"Yes," agreed Dr. Ruth.

Hugh felt a pinch in his hind leg again and soon he drifted into unconsciousness.

"I think he will be alright," Dr. Ruth said.

"Yes, three or four weeks off that foot and he should be as good as new," Dr. Jim responded. "We better get him into his sling before he wakes up. He will feel better hanging in mid-air than strapped down like this."

When Hugh woke up again, he was hanging off the ground. He looked about at his new, strange surroundings. He saw other animals walking and limping around. They were as calm as could be. Then he moved his legs and he swung slowly back and forth but did not touch the ground. The humans were close by and approached.

"Hi, do you like your new bed?" one asked. They both petted him. Hugh liked that. It felt just like when his mother nuzzled him. Then he remembered his mother told him that humans wouldn't hurt him.

Then they put something in his mouth. He tried to resist but they forced it in. Soon he realized he was drinking water. It tasted so good. He had such a thirst.

"There, isn't that good?" a soothing voice asked.

Hugh drank the whole bottle. Then they gave him grass to eat. As he chomped, he looked about. Yes, all the animals seemed to be calm and relaxed, Hugh observed. This must be a safe place. But he wondered where his mother was.

Every day the humans visited Hugh. They gave him food and water and inspected his foot but they did not let him down. But Hugh got used to his sling and enjoyed being suspended in mid-air. It was really quite comfortable. Sometimes one of the other animals would come and sniff at one of Hugh's feet and then it would go on its way. Then, one day Dr. Ruth and Dr. Jim came and took the white stuff off of Hugh's foot.

"Looks good," Dr. Jim said as his firm, steady hands explored the uncovered foot. "I'll hold him and you loosen the sling."

Dr. Jim put his arms around Hugh and held him firmly as Dr. Ruth loosened the sling. Then Dr. Jim eased Hugh to the ground. He did not let Hugh go right away but allowed Hugh's weight to rest on his four feet. When he was firmly planted, Dr. Jim released his hold.

Hugh stood for a moment, remembering how painful it was to walk. But now his foot didn't hurt. He pawed the ground a bit and then took a step. The Doctors watched closely, ready to lift Hugh if he showed any signs of distress.

Hugh took a step and then another. Soon his walk went to a slow trot. Hugh threw his head up and began to prance around the enclosure. The Doctors congratulated each other as they watched Hugh move around the pen.

"He looks ready to go," Dr. Ruth smiled.

"OK. Tomorrow we'll take him back to the herd and see if he finds his mother."

"Even if he doesn't, he is old enough to forage for himself," Dr. Ruth noted.

Hugh was left to roam around the pen and eat and drink as much as he wanted. Now he was anxious to get back to his mother and his friends. He had so much to tell them. He wondered how he could get over this obstacle that enclosed them all and find the plains again.

The next day the humans came and gave Hugh a pinch in his hind leg and he was asleep again. When he started to wake up, he was being carried out of the strange thing the humans sat in. They laid him on the grass and backed away. Soon Hugh was fully awake and rose quickly to his feet. Not far away was the whole Gnu herd, grazing as peacefully as could be.

Hugh raced to join them. The Gnus momentarily paused from their grazing and stared at Hugh racing towards them. "Mother! Mother!" he called. But where could she be in this vast herd? He would run through the whole herd until he found her, he told himself.

But in only a few minutes, Hugh and his mother were reunited with many licks and many nuzzles. Hugh raced all around her and kicked up his heels with delight.

Dr. Jim put his arm around Dr. Ruth's shoulder.

"I hope he has a full, happy life," Dr. Ruth sighed.

"He's off to a good start," Dr. Jim commented.

The two watched the herd until late afternoon. Then they got into their Rover and headed back to camp. There were many other animals to rescue and tomorrow would be another day.

THE END

MALCOLM THE BUNNY

Malcolm peeked out of his den which was nestled deep in the woods. The ground was all white.

"Mother, Mother," Malcolm called excitedly. "Come and see! The ground is all white!"

Malcolm's mother hopped over and peered out. "Yes," she said. "It is winter and that is snow."

"Snow?" echoed Malcolm.

You see, Malcolm was just a baby bunny and he had never seen snow before. In fact, he had never been more than a few feet from the door to his den. He was too young to venture far.

"Snow," repeated his mother. "In the summer there is rain. Remember the rains?"

"Yes," Malcolm replied.

"Well, in the winter the rain becomes little white flakes. We call that snow. Instead of getting the ground all wet, it blankets the ground and makes it all white."

"Can I hop on it?" Malcolm asked.

"Yes," his mother smiled. "But stay right in front of our nest. Daddy and I are going to find something to eat."

"I will," Malcolm promised and he slowly proceeded through the entrance of his nest.

He was barely out of the nest, sniffing and feeling with his paws, when his parents hopped out.

"We'll be back soon," his father said. "We will bring you something good to eat. Stay right in front, now."

"I will. Bye Mom! Bye, Dad!" he called.

"Bye, son," they called back and soon they had hopped out of sight, leaving their tracks in the snow.

Malcolm liked the way this snow felt. It was nice and soft and so white. Soon he was hopping quickly and diving into snow banks. This is fun, he thought.

Well, Malcolm was having such a good time that he didn't notice that he was getting farther and farther from home. There was so much to see and so much snow to play in. And guess what? It began to snow. Big white flakes came drifting down. At first Malcolm was puzzled about this white stuff falling from the sky. Then he realized that it was more snow. It came down just like rain, only much slower and it was prettier and ever so quiet.

Malcolm jumped up to bite the flakes as they came drifting down. It was fun! And the flakes melted in his mouth, giving him a drink. But now Malcolm was getting tired. I think I will go home, he decided. Maybe Mom and Dad will be home with something good to eat. But when he turned and looked about, he realized that he was not in front of his home. In fact, nothing was familiar to him.

"My gosh!" he exclaimed. "Where am I? I think I came from that way."

But by now, the snow had covered up all of his tracks. The snow had covered up everything. Malcolm realized he was lost. Now he was scared. He hopped a little this way and then that way but he could not tell if he was going in the right direction.

Malcolm felt like crying. And he did. He sat right down in the snow and cried. And then a mother possum came hurrying by with seven of her children.

Malcolm called out, "Please, can you help me? I am lost."

"We can't stop now," the possum said as she hurried by. "Your mother will be coming soon."

Then they were gone and Malcolm was alone again. He started to cry. But he stopped when he heard a large animal crashing through the woods. Soon a large elk came into view.

Malcolm called out, "Please, can you help me? I am lost."

"I can't stop now," the elk snorted. "Your mother will be coming soon." And he lumbered off.

Malcolm sat down and cried some more. Then he heard a voice.

"You are Malcolm, aren't you?"

Malcolm looked around but he saw no one.

"I know your parents," the voice said.

"In fact I know just about everyone and everything in this forest," he boasted.

The voice seemed to be coming from above so Malcolm looked up. And there was an owl, sitting on a tree limb.

"You do?" Malcolm asked hopefully. "Do you know where I live?"

"Certainly," the owl snapped. "Don't you know that owls know everything?"

"Oh, yes, I forgot," replied Malcolm, apologetically. "Can you tell me how to get home?"

"Yes," replied the owl, in a friendlier tone.

Then he flew to another tree and landed on a limb. He turned to face Malcolm. "This way," he instructed.

Malcolm hopped quickly until he was right below the owl. Then the owl flew to another tree and waited as Malcolm caught up to him. Finally, the owl stopped on a limb and pointed with his wing, "There is your home."

Malcolm was very excited and hopped as fast as he could. Now he recognized where he was.

"Thank you," he called over his shoulder.

And there was his mother, waiting anxiously in front of the nest. She was very relieved to see her son. Malcolm rushed up to her and snuggled against her soft fur.

"Where have you been?" his mother scolded. "Your father and I have been very worried. He is out looking for you right now."

Malcolm felt sad to know that he made his parents worry so.

"Oh, mother," he exclaimed, "I was having so much fun playing in the snow that I got lost. And a nice owl showed me the way home. He said he knew you and Dad."

Mrs. Rabbit smiled and nodded. "Yes, he has lived in the woods a long time. He knows everyone in the woods. It was nice of him to help you. did you thank him?"

"Yes, mother, I remembered to thank him."

Just then, Mr. Rabbit hopped into view. He was also very happy to see Malcolm, safe and sound.

"He was having so much fun playing that he got lost," explained Mrs. Rabbit.

Mr. Rabbit nuzzled his son affectionately.

"You have to be more careful next time," he advised.

"Oh, I will," promised Malcolm.

Yes, Malcolm had learned a very important lesson. He would be very careful not to get lost again!

"Now let's go in and have some nice clover that we found under the snow," Mrs. Rabbit said. "And I will make you a nice cup of hot cocoa."

"Umm, I will like that," said Malcolm and they all hopped into their cozy home.

THE END

CHILLY THE FILLY

Chilly was only six months old. She was a pretty filly with a reddish-brown coat, a long mane and a cute, fluffy tail. Her coat was always soft and lush, her mane was neatly braided and her tail evenly trimmed. She was the nicest looking horse on the Lovely Valley Ranch which was owned by Rob and Martina, the parents of Mario and Melanie. They were twelve-year-old twins and they fell in love with Chilly as soon as she was born.

The day Chilly was born was a fateful day. Rob and Martina, Mario and Melanie and Jiminez, the foreman, were all anxiously waiting for MariBelle to deliver her first baby. MariBelle was a champion show horse and she was bred to Marvelous, a magnificent stallion. The family had high hopes for the soon-to-be-born baby.

MariBelle was a gentle, most lovable horse and always at her peak in a show. She really belonged to Martina but everyone loved her. She seemed to know when she was competing and moved and posed to perfection. She wasn't going to let any of those other horses outdo her. And they seldom did!

Her coat, tail and yellow mane were beautiful and she always held her head up high. But when she was eight, Rob and Martina decided to retire MariBelle from competition. They felt it was time to breed her and let her start a family.

Marvelous, a fiery stallion and champion in his own right, belonged to a neighbor. He was already retired a year when it was decided to breed him to MariBelle. Both owners thought the prospects for an excellent offspring were very high. So all concerned waited impatiently for MariBelle to deliver her first foal, hopefully the first of many. They waited impatiently most of the scheduled day.

"Let's have some supper," Martina suggested, "I'm starving."

"Good idea," said Rob. "We need a break."

The children resisted, afraid they would miss the big moment.

"But if MariBelle delivers, no one will be here to help her," objected Melanie.

"We won't even be gone an hour," Martina answered. "Nothing will happen in an hour. And Jiminez is here."

The children followed their parents to the house, reluctantly. They wolfed down their sandwiches, potato chips and milk and begged to be excused.

Rob and Martina smiled. "OK," they said. "We will be along in a minute."

With that, the children jumped from their chairs and ran out. In a minute they were both screaming for their parents to come. That could only mean one thing - MariBelle was delivering!

"Oh my gosh!" Rob reacted, "MariBelle must be foaling!"

Rob and Martina rushed out of the house and into the barn. Jiminez was already there. When they got to the foaling stall, MariBelle was standing quietly with a most beautiful foal right beside her.

"Oh, look!" Martina whispered, with the feelings that only a mother could know after the miracle of birth. "Isn't she beautiful?"

Suddenly the baby shook her head, gave a little whinny and kicked up her hind legs. With that she lost her balance and flopped down on her rump!

Everyone laughed at this little clown.

She quickly struggled to her feet and hurried to the safety of her mother.

"I think she is a little embarrassed," laughed Mario!

"She has a lot of her father's fire," Rob remarked.

"Oh, she is going to be a little pepper pot," Jiminez exclaimed.

"Yes, she is," Melanie added. "Let's call her Chilly!"

"Yes," agreed Mario.

"Oh, I don't know," Martina puzzled. "Does that sound like a good name for a show horse?"

"Oh, please, mom," the children cried, jumping up and down and hugging her.

"We can register her in another name," Rob whispered to his wife. "Let them call her Chilly. Her red coat looks like chili peppers. It is suitable!"

"OK," Martina agreed.

The children laughed with excitement and were soon grooming and pampering the new baby.

MariBelle looked on trustingly and waited for her turn. Even though she was retired, she still enjoyed looking her best and appreciated the nice feelings she had when being brushed and curried.

And a pepper pot Chilly was. She couldn't wait to be led into the pasture in the morning. She raced around, kicking up her heels and snorting. Sometimes she got so carried away that she would bump into her mother. MariBelle would give her a nip on her hind quarters, letting her know she should be careful. But Chilly didn't mind her mother's little nips and would immediately run off.

On one morning, Chilly was standing close to her mother's side but she was watching for the children. She knew they always had something good to eat and Chilly was always in the mood for a treat. There were several apple trees on the farm so there was usually an abundance of apples for the horses, as well as for Martina's delicious pies and tarts for Rob and the children.

Sure enough, here they came. Chilly took off for the fence. MariBelle followed at a leisurely pace. She knew she would get a treat and saw no need to hurry. Most of the other horses meandered over to the fence for a treat, seeming to have a "plenty-for-all" attitude.

The children greeted Chilly loudly and petted her head and neck as she stretched for apples. Then it was time for her grooming.

Now Chilly was a year old and Rob and Martina looked her over with experienced eyes.

"I don't think she has it," Rob said, disappointedly.

"It looks that way but maybe she will still develop," Martina responded.

33

But she didn't sound very enthusiastic.

"Maybe. We'll see," answered Rob.

There didn't seem to be another MariBelle show horse in Chilly. They turned and walked towards the house. Chilly watched them go.

But in a few months, there was a noticeable change in the confirmation of Chilly. She actually grew into a beautiful young horse. Rob and Martina found it hard to believe. There was definitely show-quality in their baby.

"To think that we had all but written her off," Martina said to Rob.

"She certainly got a growth spurt. I think we have a competitor here," Rob smiled.

"I'm going to start training her so she will be ready for the two-year-old competition. I'm going to get the children involved, too," Martina added. "Let's tell them."

"Good idea. It's time they started learning the business."

Chilly responded well to the rigorous training necessary to win in competition. Rob, Martina and Jiminez were impressed. The children were excited.

"She is a natural," Martina remarked.

"Takes after her parents and she has the best trainer in the whole world," Rob teased.

Martina laughed but enjoyed the compliment.

As the day of the competition neared, the excitement increased. They would have to drive Chilly two hundred miles in the horse trailer. To prepare her, Rob and Martina loaded her into the enclosed trailer and drove short distances.

At first Chilly didn't want to get into the trailer. Rob and Jiminez held tightly to the rope attached to her halter. She reared and whinnied and pulled. She was afraid!

Then Mario and Melanie stood inside the trailer and called to her, holding out carrots and apples. Chilly stood very still for a moment, listening to the children call her. She stared inside the trailer and could see them. She also saw the treats in their hands.

Soon she pranced right up the ramp and into the trailer and gobbled her treats while the children hugged her neck. Jiminez tied the end of the rope securely and the trailer gate was raised and locked.

With Jiminez and the children in the trailer with Chilly, Rob started the pickup and slowly moved forward. After he knew Chilly was comfortable, he increased speed and soon was going fifty-miles-per-hour down the highway. Chilly was as calm as could be and the children laughed, petted and praised her all the way.

Three days before the show date, Martina loaded Chilly and the children into the trailer and set out for Hendron where the Fair was being held. Martina wanted to get there a little early so Chilly could get used to her new surroundings. Jiminez came but Rob stayed home to run the farm.

During the drive, something was on Martina's mind, something she had been thinking about for a while. Just before she reached The Hendron Fair Gounds, she made up her mind. Mario and Melanie would show Chilly. Martina had listed both their names as trainers, along with hers, so there would be no problems with the judges.

Why not, she thought. It's only Chilly's first show. If she needs a stronger hand, I can step in at the next meet. Yes, this is the right thing to do and the right time, she assured herself.

Chilly was glad to be out of the trailer after the eight-hour drive and was very curious about her new surroundings. Where was the familiar barn and pasture and who were all of these strange horses? But she seemed to readily adjust and was relaxed with plenty of hay and oats and her familiar caretakers.

During dinner, Martina told the children that they would show Chilly. At first they were excited but then they became apprehensive.

"Gosh, mom, what if we make Chilly do something wrong?" Melanie questioned.

Martina answered, "You two have been working with Chilly for six months. You have watched me train horses for years. You know what to do and Chilly knows what to do. Don't worry about making a mistake! All trainers make mistakes! I have made plenty. Chilly is young enough to be in many shows so if she doesn't win this one, there will be others!"

The children were relieved but they were still aware of their responsibility.

The morning of the show, the children were dressed in their nicest riding outfits and Chilly was as pretty as a picture. Her mane was braided and ribboned, her tail had pretty little bows, her coat was flawless and her white bridle complimented the color of her coat. Martina took several pictures of the children with Chilly so Rob could see how they looked. Jiminez beamed with pride.

Mario and Melanie worked well together, putting Chilly through her paces and Chilly responded immediately to their commands. The expressions on the faces of the judges gave no clue as to which horses they favored.

Finally the judges were ready to announce the winners. Martina, the children and Jiminez waited anxiously for the eternity to end and the ribbons awarded.

"First Prize goes to . . . PRETTY-IN-BLUE!"

Cheers and applause broke out but for Chilly's little group there was big disappointment. Martina felt sorry for the children and Melanie fought to hold back her tears. Even Mario wanted to cry.

"Second Prize goes to . . . MARIBELLE'S BABY!

Martina and Jiminez jumped for joy! Fortunately they were off to the side so no one noticed. Mario and Melanie smiled broadly and accepted the ribbon. Chilly knew she had done something and pranced for the crowd, which applauded and laughed.

Martina phoned Rob right away with the good news and the four sang most of the way home. Chilly got extra oats and lots of praises and pats, which was all she wanted. She was a natural in the show ring and Martina was sure she would win many prizes before her career was over.

Rob was waiting for them when they arrived home. After lots of hugs and laughter, Chilly was turned loose in the pasture where she quickly ran to her mother. MariBelle snorted a greeting.

"I think the judges were swayed because Pretty-in-Blue was a local horse. Otherwise Chilly would have won First Prize," Martina declared. Jiminez nodded in agreement.

Everyone laughed! It was a good feeling to have a wonderful horse and to all be together.

Everyone slept well that night, even Chilly who dreamed of getting apples and carrots from Mario and Melanie the first thing in the morning.

THE END

PETER THE PIG

Peter the pig woke up early. He jumped out of bed and looked out of his window. It was going to be a beautiful day to go to the market. He washed his hands and face and dressed with great anticipation. After a bowl of pig cereal and a glass of milk, Peter got his grocery list and grocery cart and skipped out the front door.

As he walked along, he reviewed his grocery list. There was celery, carrots, milk, eggs, cereal, lettuce, tomatoes and bread. Notice there was no ham or bacon on Peter's list. Peter never ate ham or bacon.

Peter had not gone very far when he came upon his neighbor Logan the Loon. Logan was standing by the side of the road, looking very sad.

"Hi, Logan! Why are you so sad?" Peter asked.

"Look, my wagon is broken. Can you help me fix it?"

"I don't have time now," answered Peter. "I am on my way to the market. Perhaps when I return."

And he walked right past his neighbor Logan.

Soon he came upon his friend Robert the rabbit. Robert was standing by the side of the road, looking very sad.

"Hi, Robert! Why are you looking so sad?" asked Peter.

"Look, my bicycle has a flat tire. Can you help me fix it?"

"I don't have time now," answered Peter. "I am on my way to the market. Perhaps when I return."

And he walked right past his friend Robert.

Soon he came upon his co-worker Patty the porcupine. Patty was standing by the side of the road, looking very sad.

"Hi, Patty! Why are you looking so sad?" asked Peter.

Look, the heel of my shoe is unglued. Can you help me fix it?"

"I don't have time now," answered Peter. "I am on my way to the market. Perhaps when I return."

And he walked right past his co-worker Patty. Then Peter arrived at the market and he purchased all of his groceries. The clerk put them all in three bags and Peter happily placed the bags in his cart. When all was ready, he headed for home, pulling his cart behind him.

He did not get too far when one of the wheels of his cart came off. Try as he may, Peter could not get the wheel to stay on. Oh, this was so inconvenient, he thought. So he set his cart by a tree, took his three bags of groceries and began to carry them home. As he walked, the bags got heavier and heavier.

"I wish I had someone to help me carry these bags," he said aloud.

Soon he saw his co-worker Patty the porcupine walking by the side of the road. "There is Patty," Peter said. "She will help me. Patty!" he called. "My cart lost its wheel. Can you help me carry my groceries home?"

"I can't. My shoe is still broken," Patty answered. "I can't walk very well. Perhaps another time."

Peter struggled on and then he saw his friend Robert the rabbit. "There is Robert," Peter said. "He will help me. Robert!" he called. "My cart lost its wheel. Can you help me carry my groceries home?

"I can't," answered Robert. "I have to fix my bike. Perhaps another time."

Peter struggled on and then he saw his neighbor Logan the Loon. "There is Logan," Peter said. "He will help me. Logan!" he called. "My cart lost its wheel. Can you help me carry my groceries home?"

"I can't," Logan answered. "I have to fix my wagon. Perhaps another time."

Peter struggled on, finally reaching his home. He placed his three heavy bags on his kitchen table and breathed a sigh or relief.

"Phew!" he gasped. "I made it."

He collapsed on a chair to catch his breath. As he sat resting, he began to think. If I had helped my friends with their problems, they could have helped me with my problem. The next time I see someone who needs help, I am going to help them if I can and not just think about myself, Peter resolved.

Then he got up and put away all of his groceries and made a fine sandwich and poured a glass of milk for his lunch. After lunch, he picked up his tool box and went to fetch his cart.

As he walked, he saw his neighbor Logan the Loon. "Hi, Logan," Peter called.

"Hi, Peter," Logan responded. "Where are you going?"

"I'm going to fix the wheel on my cart," Peter answered.

"Put your tool box in my wagon and I will go with you."

"OK," answered Peter. He placed his tool box in the wagon and the two walked along together.

"I feel much better without carrying that heavy tool box," Peter said. "Thank you."

"You are welcome," Logan replied.

Soon they came upon Robert the rabbit. "Hi," he called. "Where are you two going?"

"We're going to fix my cart," answered Peter.

"Why don't you tie the handle of your wagon to my bike and I will pull it?" offered Robert.

"That's a swell idea," said Logan. So they tied the handle to Robert's bike and the three went on together.

Soon they came upon Patty the porcupine who had gone home and changed her shoes. "Where are you all going?" she asked.

"We are going to fetch my cart," answered Peter. "My tool box is in Logan's wagon and Robert is pulling it on his bike."

"May I walk with you?" asked Patty. "Maybe I can help."

"Sure," answered Peter. "You are most welcome."

So they all walked along together and chatted about this and that and even sang a song. When they reached Peter's cart, they had it fixed in no time.

Then they all went back to Peter's house and he made a pitcher of lemonade and served homemade cookies. Everyone had a swell time and enjoyed being friends forever.

"It sure is nice to have such good friends," Peter remarked.

Everyone agreed!

THE END

HARREY THE BUNNY

It was Spring, that was for sure. The days were getting warmer and all through the forest things were getting greener and greener. Harrey could hardly wait to get out and eat some of the wonderful plants and grasses that were sprouting.

Harrey's parents were the first to leave the nest. Harrey and his brothers and sisters waited impatiently for permission to come out. Mr. and Mrs. Rabbit hopped out cautiously, looking about and sniffing the air for signs of danger. When they were sure it was safe, they called the children. All hopped out as quickly as possible and soon they were all munching clover, sweet shoots and tender petals.

"Ummm, this is delicious," Harrey said to Bonnie, his sister who was close by.

"Ooh, yes," she replied between bites. "Try this!"

Harrey hopped over and nibbled. "Ummm," he sighed.

Once everyone had eaten their fill, Harrey and his brothers and sisters began to romp about. They chased each other through the tall grass and around the trees. Everyone was laughing and tumbling about.

"Come on," whispered Harrey to Bonnie, "let's explore."

"Do you think it's safe?" she asked timidly.

"Sure. We won't go far," he promised.

"OK," Bonnie agreed. And off they hopped.

Soon Harrey and Bonnie came upon two baby ferrets. They had never seen ferrets before and stopped to stare. The ferrets had never seen rabbits before so they stared back. They approached each other cautiously.

"Hi," said Harrey. "My name is Harrey and this is my sister Bonnie. What are your names?"

"My name is Kerry," said one ferret.

"And my name is Berry," said the other. "What kind of animals are you?"

"We're rabbits," answered Bonnie. "What kind are you?"

"We're ferrets," replied Berry.

"Where do you live?" asked Harrey.

"Near that tree," said Kerry.

"We live in a nest under the ground," said Bonnie, "but it's more fun being outside."

"Yes, much more fun" responded the ferrets. "Want to play?"

"Yes," replied Harrey and Bonnie.

"Let's play hide-and-seek," said Berry. "One of us will be the fox and the rest of us will have to run and hide."

"OK," replied Harrey and Bonnie. They had never played hide-and-seek before but it sounded like fun.

"I'll be the fox," said Kerry. "I'll count to ten. You hide and I will try to find you."

Kerry closed his eyes began to count out loud, "One, two, three . . ."

Everyone hurried to find a good hiding place. This was exciting!

". . . Nine and ten! Here I come, ready or not," called Kerry.

Kerry hurried about, quickly going here and there, searching for his hidden friends. He found Harrey first and tagged him. "Got you!" he shouted.

This is fun, Harrey thought. Bonnie and Berry remained in their hiding places, quivering with anticipation.

Suddenly Kerry jumped on Bonnie's back, shouting, "I've got you! I've got you!"

Bonnie squealed with excitement as she rolled away from Kerry. Then Harrey and Berry jumped on them and the four rolled around in the grass, laughing and jostling each other.

"This game is fun," said Harrey and Bonnie.

"It's our favorite," said Berry.

Before they could start another game, a voice was heard, "Kerry, Berry."

"Oh, it's Mom," said Kerry. "We have to go."

"Oh," said Harrey and Bonnie, disappointed that the fun had to end.

"Let's meet tomorrow and we can play some more," said the ferrets.

"Oh, yes," said Harrey and Bonnie.

"OK, tomorrow," said the ferrets.

"Yes," agreed Harrey and Bonnie.

"Bye," said Kerry and Berry.

Then they turned and hurried away just as their mother called again.

Bonnie and Harrey called "Good-bye" and watched their new friends disappear in the tall grass. They were a little sad to see Kerry and Berry go away.

"I think it's time to go home, too," said Harrey.

"OK," said Bonnie and the two turned and hopped away.

When they neared their home, they saw their mother. She was starting to look for them.

"Where have you two been?" she scolded.

"Oh, Mom, we met some ferrets," answered Harrey.

"And we played hide-and-seek. It was a swell game," added Bonnie.

Mrs. Rabbit could see how happy her children were so she didn't want to scold too much.

"I'm glad you had fun but you must always tell me when you are going somewhere. There is always danger in the forest. Now it is almost dark. See?"

"OK, Mom," they answered.

"We're sorry, Mom," said Bonnie. "Can we play with the ferrets tomorrow?"

"I think it will be alright but we shall see," Mrs. Rabbit replied. "Now it's time to come home."

Mrs. Rabbit led her two children safely back to the nest. Now everyone was home. The other children were half asleep already. Mr. Rabbit was happy to see his two children were safe. He was a little worried, too.

Harrey and Bonnie snuggled up with their brothers and sisters and were warm and cozy. It had been a long day. They were tired and glad to be home. It would be good to sleep.

"Tomorrow I will be the fox," whispered Bonnie.

"You won't find me," Harrey whispered back.

"Yes I will," she answered and gave her brother a poke with her front paw. Harrey giggled softly.

"Will not," he teased.

"Shhh!" scolded Mrs. Rabbit.

"Will too," Bonnie hissed in her brother's furry ear.

"Quiet!" said Mr. Rabbit, in his firm tone. That meant business!

Harrey and Bonnie quickly settled down and soon everyone was fast asleep.

Yes, Harrey and Bonnie dreamed of playing hide-and-seek with Kerry and Berry.

THE END

ABNER THE BURRO

Did you know that long ago in a land so far away lived a burro? Abner was his name!

Abner was a poor orphan! His parents had been caught by the farmers and led off to work. Little Abner was very frightened when the farmers came on their horses, swinging their lassos.

"Run!" cried Abner's mother, when she saw the farmers coming. "Run to the river!"

Abner put his ears back and ran off, just as his mother told him. He didn't see his mother and father run in a different direction. They did this so the farmers would chase them instead of little Abner.

Their plan worked. The farmers didn't see Abner as his parents were in plain sight, almost daring the farmers to chase them.

"After them!" shouted one of the farmers and three horsemen took off in pursuit.

It didn't take long for the horses to overtake Abner's parents. The lassos whistled through the air and caught one and then the other. With ropes around their necks, Abner's parents were led off with little resistance.

Abner reached the river which was lined with trees, affording many hiding places. "We made it! We made it!" Abner panted but then he realized his parents were not with him. He turned and retraced his steps, looking this way and that and calling softly. Soon he saw the men riding and laughing. Then he saw his parents with ropes around their necks.

"Oh, Mother, Father," he cried softly.

He followed them at a safe distance. After a while, he saw fields of corn and some white buildings. He remembered this place! Sometimes he would come with his parents and eat delicious corn.

"If you hear the men coming with their horses," Abner's mother warned, "run to the river!"

"I will," Abner answered, not really understanding why he had to run.

Abner did not go any further once he recognized the field. He found a nice grassy place under a big shady tree and lay down to rest. He was tired!

When it was dark, he would look for his parents. Soon he dozed and woke to see a full moon and many stars. It was night!

He started towards the buildings where his parents probably were. The corn was high enough to hide him as he walked quietly between the rows. He ate three ears of that delicious corn as he walked and then came to the end of the field. He peeked out. Close by was a fenced place and some horses stood dozing peacefully behind the white boards.

Then, in one corner of the fenced place Abner saw his parents standing close together. Abner's heart leapt for joy! He was so glad to see them. He approached carefully until the white fence rails were all that separated him from his parents.

"Mother, Father," he whispered.

Their ears pricked up and they looked about alertly.

"Here I am," Abner whispered.

His parents saw him and moved to the fence. They put their heads between the fence rails and nuzzled their baby. They were all delighted to be together again.

"Can you come out?" asked Abner.

"No," replied his father. "The fence is too strong and too high."

Abner felt like crying.

"Then I shall hide in the corn and come to see you every night," he said with determination.

"You will be caught," his mother told him anxiously. "Go back to the river. There is water and grass. You will grow up and find some other burros to be with."

"No!" Abner said, raising his voice a little. The sound stirred one of the horses. "I want to be with you," he whispered.

"Listen to us," said his father. "You must not stay here. You will be caught."

"No!" retorted Abner. "I will come back tomorrow night."

He turned and crept away before they could say any more. When he reached the corn field, he got an idea. He pulled off two ears of corn and brought them to his parents who were still watching him. He laid them just under the lowest fence rail.

"See you tomorrow," he whispered.

When he felt well hidden, he lay down to sleep. It had been a long day and he soon fell asleep, munching an ear of corn.

In the morning he woke. As soon as he opened his eyes, he saw a small man standing right in front of him. It really wasn't a small man, it was a boy. Abner froze.

"Hello, little burro," the boy said softly. "My name is Pedro. Can we be friends?" Pedro held out an ear of corn to Abner.

Abner stood up and looked intently at the boy. He seemed like a nice little man, Abner thought. He took the corn and began to eat. Pedro touched Abner's head and petted him.

"You are a nice burro," Pedro said as he rubbed Abner's head and neck. Abner liked that.

"I will call you Abner," the boy said.

Abner wondered how the boy knew his name.

Pedro took a short rope from his belt and tied one end around Abner's neck. Then he tugged the other end of the rope gently and Abner walked along with his new friend.

Pedro led Abner out of the corn field and towards one of the white buildings. Abner looked for his parents as he walked but they were not inside the fenced place.

When they reached the building which was Pedro's house, Pedro stopped.

"Mamasita," he called.

Soon a dark-haired lady, short and stocky, came through the door.

"Look what I found," Pedro called to his mother. "May I keep him?"

Pedro's mother was surprised. Her son found a burro?

"Where did you find him?" she asked.

"In the corn field," replied Pedro.

She studied the pair for a moment, then said, "I guess it's OK. Show your father."

Pedro was very happy. "Thank you, Mamasita," he cried and lead Abner away.

When Abner saw the men, he reared, almost jerking the rope from Pedro's hand.

"Whoa!" called Pedro. "It's alright. This is my father. He will not harm you."

Pedro's father, Juan, and the other men looked up from their work. They were surprised to see Pedro with a little burro.

Then Abner saw his parents. They were harnessed to a wagon which was full of corn. When Abner saw them, he hurried over, almost pulling Pedro off his feet. The men laughed to see Pedro trying to restrain his burro.

Abner and his parents stood nuzzling each other.

"Where did you get this burro?" Pedro's father asked.

"I found him in the corn field," Pedro replied.

"See the way he nuzzles the other two?" mentioned one of the workers. "He must be their baby."

All the men looked.

"I think you are right," said Juan.

Then Juan examined Abner with his strong hands and looked him over with an experienced eye. Juan knew a good burro when he saw one. He nodded his head.

"He is sound," he pronounced. "OK, son, you may keep him but when he is old enough, he must work."

Pedro was delighted. "He will be a very good worker, father. You will see."

"Now," said Juan, "help us put this corn in the bin. There is much to pick yet."

Pedro left Abner with his parents and helped unload the wagon. When it was empty, Juan drove the wagon to the field where everyone picked corn and placed it in the wagon.

Abner saw how easily his parents pulled the wagon. He pranced along beside them, wishing he could help pull.

When work was done, Pedro would climb on Abner's back and ride to the big pond where they swam and played til it was time to go home for dinner.

One day Pedro was riding Abner to the pond when a big rattlesnake appeared right in front of them. Abner was startled and reared. He knew about rattlesnakes from his parents and did not want to get bitten.

The snake was coiled and ready to strike. When Abner reared, Pedro rolled right off Abner's back and hit the ground with a thud. He lay motionless while Abner stood between him and the snake, rearing and making a terrible noise.

The snake knew he was no match for Abner and he quickly slithered away.

Abner turned to see Pedro still lying on the ground. He nuzzled him gently but Pedro did not move. Abner saw a big bump on Pedro's forehead. He must be hurt, Abner thought. Maybe Pedro's father should come. Abner turned and galloped off as fast as he could.

As he approached the white house, Abner brayed loudly. Juan was sitting in his rocking chair, resting until dinner was ready. He looked up when he heard Abner braying. Abner slid to a stop in front of the porch and continued to bray.

Juan was startled by all the commotion. Some of the workers came to see what was happening and Pedro's mama came out of the house.

"What is wrong?" she asked.

"I don't know. This burro must be loco," Juan answered.

"Where is Pedro?" asked mama.

Suddenly Juan became alarmed. He stepped off the porch and grabbed Abner's bridle.

"Where is Pedro?" he asked the braying burro.

Abner snorted and pawed the ground.

"Something is wrong," said mama.

"Bring the horses," Juan ordered his men.

Soon they came running, pulling three unsaddled horses. Two of the men wanted to go with Juan. All jumped on the horses and Juan commanded Abner, "Go! Find Pedro!"

Abner spun about and raced away with Juan and his men close behind. Soon he reached the lifeless body of poor Pedro and slid to a stop, making a cloud of dust.

The men were off their horses in a flash and Juan knelt down and examined his son. He saw the big bump on his forehead and quickly moved his hands over the boy's body and limbs. The other two men peered anxiously, ready to help if needed.

Then Pedro moaned. Juan slowly sat the boy up and let him rest against him, cradling him in his arms.

"Pedro, it's Daddy," he said softly, looking into the boy's face.

Pedro slowly opened his eyes. He was dazed at first but then recognized his father and smiled weakly.

"Where is Abner?" he asked quietly.

"He is here. See?" Abner lowered his head and nuzzled Pedro. Pedro smiled.

"Did you fall off?" Juan asked.

"There was a rattlesnake and it scared us," Pedro answered.

"How do you feel now?" asked Juan.

"My head hurts a little," Pedro answered.

"Move your arms and legs," Juan instructed.

Pedro did. Juan was pleased. Nothing seemed to be broken. Juan left Pedro sitting up and mounted his horse. He ordered his men to lift Pedro up which they did most carefully. They placed him in his father's arms and mounted their horses. Then they all rode slowly back to the house. Abner trotted along next to Juan's horse.

At the white house, Pedro's Mama and his two sisters were waiting anxiously. When Mama saw her son being carried by his father, she hurried to meet them. Juan handed Pedro down to her and she carried him into the house.

"He's alright," Juan assured her, "Just a bump on his head."

Mama put cool, wet towels on Pedro's bump and pressed firmly. Pedro was brave and did not complain. Mama smiled at her son, relieved to see him with only a few bruises.

Soon all were gathered round the table, enjoying corn fritters, rice, homemade bread and salad. Mama and Juan had wine to drink and the children had milk. Abner and his parents got oats and corn for their dinner.

A few years later, Juan let Abner's parents live peacefully on the farm without working. They deserve a rest, he told his wife. She smiled and nodded in agreement. Besides, Juan caught some other mules on the range and Abner also learned to pull the wagon. Abner's parents were not really needed for work anymore.

Abner grew to be a strong burro and loved pulling the wagon which Pedro now drove. And the two still found time to go to the big pond and swim and play. Pedro's parents delighted at seeing the two together, having so much fun.

And Abner's parents were very proud of what a good son Abner was. He would still go into the corn field and bring them corn to eat. They remembered the first time Abner had done that. It seemed like such a long time ago but it was very pleasant memory for them. One that they would cherish forever.

THE END

BABY THE ELEPHANT

Baby was a four-month old elephant who lived in Africa with her mother and several other elephants. All the elephants together are called a herd. There were mothers and their children in the herd so Baby had other elephants to play with.

Baby loved to tramp through the grass and between the tall trees, flapping her ears and trumpeting bravely. The other baby elephants liked to do that, too, and they chased each other to prove who was the leader. The mothers smiled at the antics of their children but made sure none was hurt. When the playing got too rough, one of the mothers would scold the children and make them play safely.

Baby was starting to taste tender grasses and leaves but mostly she liked her mother's warm, sweet milk. Eventually she would not need milk and would thrive on all the greens in the jungle. Elephants eat so much they must stroll through the jungles and plains for miles, finding new things to eat. Baby loved her long walks each day but at night, she would snuggle up to her mother and sleep deeply.

Baby loved to jump into a river and splash and swim. She would fill her trunk with water and splash her mother. Mombo, Baby's mother, would pretend to be surprised when Baby splashed her and Baby would laugh with delight at getting her mother wet. Baby and the other little elephants would have water fights, filling their trunks and blowing water on each other. It was great fun.

When the elephants came out of the water, they would roll in the dirt to coat their wrinkled hides with mud. This was good protection against the strong rays of the sun and made the elephants cooler as they resumed their walk.

One day bad hunters came into the jungle. It is against the law to hunt elephants but the bad hunters disobeyed the law. They wanted the ivory tusks of the elephants and they weren't going to obey the law.

A giant crow, circling high overhead, was the first to spy the hunters. He cawed loudly, warning all the animals below of impending danger. The elephant's leader understood the crow's signal and trumpeted the alarm.

"Run!" cried Mombo. "Run!"

All the elephants began to run as fast as they could. It was a stampede! Baby put her ears back and ran blindly. She was afraid. Finally, Baby could run no further. She was exhausted. She leaned against a tree and panted loudly, eventually catching her breath.

"Are we safe now, Mother?" she asked sheepishly.

Suddenly, Baby realized she was all alone, deep in the jungle. She got separated from the herd as everyone scattered.

"Mother!" she cried loudly. "Mother, here I am."

But there was no answer. The jungle was strangely quiet. Baby began to cry. She stood very still for a long time and just cried and called for her mother.

Maybe I can find her, Baby thought. So she started walking and trumpeting so her mother would hear. She walked and walked. Baby was very lost. She spent the night dozing and waking and when it was light, she started walking again. She came upon a stream and took a good, long drink. That tasted good. It made her feel better.

I will just follow this stream, she thought, and eventually I will find my mother. That thought gave her hope and she started off, trumpeting now and then so her mother could hear.

After several hours, Baby was still lost. "I'll never find her," she cried and started to sit down.

"Hey, careful! Don't sit on me!" a voice cried out.

Baby stopped and looked around. There was a little mongoose lying right where Baby was going to sit.

"I won't hurt you," Baby said.

"Thanks," said the mongoose as he got up from where he had been resting.

"My name is Chumba," said the mongoose.

"Mine is Baby."

"Nice to meet you," said Chumba.

"Nice to meet you," Baby replied. "I am lost. Have you seen a herd of elephants?" Baby asked hopefully.

"Naw," answered Chumba.

Baby began to cry.

"Aw, don't cry. I will ask my mom. Maybe she knows where your friends are," said Chumba, encouragingly.

Baby stopped crying and felt better.

"Let me jump on your head and I will show you where I live."

Baby put her trunk down and Chumba scurried up and sat down on top of Baby's head.

"OK, go straight that way," Chumba instructed.

Baby set off, clomping through the jungle at a brisk pace.

"There, see those holes in the ground over there? That's where I live. Stop right here."

Baby stopped and Chumba ran down her trunk and into a hole. Soon he emerged with his parents and many brothers and sisters.

"See, Mom, this is my friend Baby. She lost her herd."

"Dear me," declared Chumba's mother. "Well, don't worry, dear, we'll find them. Now you sit here and we'll go and hunt."

"Children," mother called, "spread out and look for Baby's herd. When you find it come right back here."

The mongoose ran off in all directions.

"Don't worry, honey, they'll find them."

Baby smiled.

"Now you eat some of this nice grass," ordered Mrs. Mongoose. "You look hungry."

Mothers know when children are hungry. Baby began to eat. My, yes, she was hungry indeed. Soon she filled her empty stomach and forgot about her troubles for a while.

Soon Chumba came running back. "We found them! We found them!" he exclaimed excitedly. "The monkeys told us where they were."

Baby squealed with delight.

"OK, Chumba," his mother instructed. "You take Baby to her herd and then you come right back here. Do you understand?"

"Yes, Mama," Chumba answered as he climbed Baby's trunk and took his position on her head. "That way," he called to Baby.

Baby started to run, trumpeting loudly. Soon she heard the familiar call of her mother. Baby answered as loud as she could and her mother heard her. At a clearing, Baby saw the herd, lazing about and eating grass. Her mother was at the edge of the herd with her trunk raised high. She called to Baby and Baby answered. She began to race towards her mother.

"Wait!" cried Chumba. "Let me down!"

Baby had forgotten all about Chumba and she stopped abruptly when she heard him cry out. Chumba rolled down Baby's trunk, into the soft grass.

"Oh, thank you, Chumba," Baby cried.

"You're welcome," said Chumba. Then he turned and hurried home, just like his mother had instructed.

Baby waved good-bye then turned to meet her mother who was thundering towards her.

It was a happy meeting and soon the other mothers and their children came to greet Baby. None had been shot by the bad hunters. Baby was glad. And poor Mombo was worried that her Baby had been shot!

After Baby had a long drink of milk, the herd began its slow trek through the jungle.

Baby was so happy to be with her mother and her friends that she didn't know what to do with herself. She frisked about, touching all the elephants with her little trunk.

After they had walked for a while, Mombo told Baby that they were coming to a river soon. "We can have a nice swim," Mombo said. "And no splashing mother," she chided.

But Baby knew she was just teasing. She would give her mother a good splash when they got to the river and her mother would scream with surprise. Baby could hardly wait til they got to the river. It would be such fun.

THE END

HERMIE THE SQUIRREL

Did you know that long ago in a land so far away, there lived a squirrel in a large oak tree? Hermie was the squirrel's name and his nest was made of nice, soft leaves and bits of rabbit fur. At night, Hermie would curl up in his nest and use his fluffy tail for a blanket. He would fall to sleep listening to the sounds of the forest - the rustling of the leaves, the rippling of the brook and sometimes a night bird singing a pretty song.

In the morning, Hermie got up and scampered down the oak tree and hunted for acorns and wild berries. Then he would take a nice drink from the brook where the water was always cool and tasty.

Then he'd play with his friends, other squirrels, rabbits and chipmunks and a raccoon and even a couple of skunks. He also liked to watch the birds fly from tree to tree and hop on the ground, looking for things to eat. Everyone ate and played for most of the day but when the sun began to set, they all scampered home to their nests.

"Goodbye," they called, as they turned for home. "See you in the morning."

And sure enough, in the morning everyone came out and had a fine time.

One morning Hermie woke up and it seemed awfully quiet. Hermie couldn't figure out what was so different but it just wasn't the same. He peeked out of his nest and looked down to the ground. Everything looked the same. Then he climbed down from his tree, a little more cautiously than usual. When he reached the ground, he still could find nothing wrong.

Some of his friends were already scampering about, looking for breakfast. Hermie began looking, too. He found a nice acorn and several wild raspberries. Ummmm, they were good, he thought. Then he hurried towards the brook for a nice, cool drink.

As he neared the brook, he noticed that it wasn't rippling. That's what's missing, he said to himself.

"Hey, everybody," he called. "The brook's not rippling."

Everyone stopped scampering about and listened. Sure enough, not a ripple.

"Come on," Hermie cried. "Let's find out what's wrong."

So everyone hurried to the brook. And when they got there, they were all surprised.

"Why, it's almost dry," exclaimed Hermie.

"Yes," said the skunk, "It's almost dry."

"What could have happened?" asked the rabbit.

"I don't know but let's find out," replied Hermie.

Then he began to run along the path the brook usually followed, with all the other animals right behind. Soon they all came to a stop and stood with their mouths open.

"Look," called Hermie. "Someone has dammed up the brook. That's why the water isn't flowing."

"Yes, you are right," agreed the raccoon.

They all hurried up to the little dam for a closer look. "Oh, I see," said the rabbit. "These sticks just got jammed together and made a dam. All the water is being held back by all these sticks and leaves and stuff."

"Yes, it's just a tangle of stuff," said the chipmunk.

"Let's untangle this mess so the water can flow and we can all drink again."

"Oh, yes," they all agreed.

Then they rushed at the twigs and leaves and pulled them with their sharp teeth and scratched at them with their paws.

Soon the tangle was all undone and the water rushed forward. Everyone cheered.

"Now we have our rippling brook and we can have all the water we want."

"Hooray!" they shouted and scampered along the rippling brook.

That night when Hermie snuggled in his nest and covered himself with his fluffy tail, he cocked his ear and listened. Sure enough, he heard the rippling brook. All was well and then he fell fast asleep.

THE END

LANA THE LLAMA

Lana the Llama lived high in the Andes Mountains in Peru. She was a happy young Llama who lived with her parents and other Llamas. They roamed freely up and down the steep mountains, eating lush grasses, drinking cool mountain water and enjoying the crisp air which ruffled their fur.

As winter approached, the Llamas gradually descended to the foothills where the snow didn't cover the ground. Lana liked coming down from the mountain because she got to see people and the houses they lived in. Lana was curious about the people even though her parents warned her not to get close to them.

"Why?" she asked.

"Because the people like to catch us and make us carry their bundles and shave our fur so they can make clothes for themselves," her mother answered for the tenth time.

"Oh," answered Lana. But she liked the people anyway, especially the little ones.

One day Lana wandered away from the herd. She was so busy eating grass that she did not notice that she had strayed. Pretty soon she came to a stone wall. The people built these walls along the roads and around their houses.

"Why?" asked Lana.

"To keep animals away," her mother told her, for the tenth time.

"Oh."

Lana pulled up a mouthful of delicious grass and lifted her head to chew it. As she did, she peered over the wall. There were two of the little ones, struggling with a large bundle of sticks. Why, the bundle was much too large for those two little ones, Lana thought.

"Let's try again," the boy said, exasperatedly.

"OK," the girl said.

The two got on each end of the large bundle and stooped, grasping it with their little hands.

"OK, one, two, threeee..." the boy gasped.

With much effort, the two little ones lifted the large bundle several inches off the ground and then they proceeded down the road. But they didn't get very far and it slipped from their grasp, landing with a crash on the dirt road.

"Darn!" cried the little boy. "It's too heavy. We will never get it home."

The little girl began to cry. "But mama needs this wood to cook and make our house warm."

"I know," the little boy consoled.

With that Lana asked, "May I help you?"

The two little ones looked up in surprise. "Who are you?" asked the little boy.

"I am Lana. What are your names?"

"My name is Fernando and this is my sister Marita."

The two children stared at the Llama in disbelief. Why, their jaws even dropped as they stood in the middle of the road, staring.

"It's nice to meet you," Lana said. "That is such a large bundle you have."

"Yes, it's wood that we burn in our home for cooking and heating," answered Marita.

"Will you help us carry it? We have a long way to go and soon it will be dark. Our father is not well and he cannot gather wood just now," added Fernando.

"I will be happy to help," replied Lana.

With that, she leaped over the wall with such ease and so swiftly that she startled the children. Then she curled her legs under her body so her back was close to the ground. She settled right next to the large bundle.

"Now," she instructed, "tip the bundle on its end so it is leaning against me."

Fernando and Marita got on one end of the large bundle and with a great effort, they tipped it right against Lana's side.

"Good," said Lana, feeling a little "ouch." "Now push it over on to my back."

"Like a teeter-totter," Marita exclaimed.

Then they pushed and lifted and grunted until the large bundle was across Lana's back.

"Good," said Lana, "but I think it will slip off when I get up."

"I have a rope," Fernando called. And sure enough, there was a rope attached to his belt. "I brought extra rope so we could tie our wood into a fine bundle," he said proudly.

Then he loosed the rope from his belt and he and Marita proceeded to lash the bundle to Lana's back.

"Is that too tight?" asked Marita.

"No," smiled Lana, with a little gasp. "Just be sure the bundle is fastened enough so it doesn't fall off."

The children went over the webbing they had made over the wood.

"I think it will be alright," Fernando said with authority.

"Yes," added Marita, "I think so, too."

With that, Lana slowly rose to her feet. The children were on either side of her, balancing the large bundle. When Lana was sure the large bundle was not going to fall off, she began to walk, slowly at first and then at a more normal pace. The children marched proudly on either side of her, each with one hand steadying the large bundle.

"Isn't this fun!" cried Marita.

"Yes," answered Fernando.

As they walked, the sun began to set. The children became a little anxious.

"I hope we get home before dark," said Fernando. "Mama will worry."

"It's not much further," exclaimed Marita. "It will only be a little bit dark."

"There is our house," called Fernando. "We are home!"

The children hurried on ahead and opened the gate for Lana who casually strode through, her large bundle was still intact.

With the children on either side of her, Lana slowly settled to the ground. By now, Mama, who had been standing in the doorway waiting for her children, was in the yard.

"What is this?" she cried.

"This is our friend Lana. She helped us carry our large bundle. Now you will have plenty of wood for the fire," Fernando said, as he and Marita untied the rope and let the sticks fall to the ground.

"This is so wonderful," cried Mama. "Thank you for helping my children."

"It was no bother," Lana smiled, as she rose to her feet. But she was glad to get that heavy weight from her back.

"Thank you," cried the children, as they hugged Lana and patted her neck.

Umm, Lana liked the hugs and pats. She had never had those before. She nuzzled each of the children affectionately.

"Wait!" called Mama, "I have just picked and washed some carrots. You will like them."

Mama hurried into the house and came out with three large carrots. Lana had never seen a carrot before and she was a little reluctant to take one in her mouth. They smell good, she thought. So she took a little nibble off the end of one carrot.

"Ummm," said Lana and soon devoured all three carrots. "Thank you," she said.

"You are welcome," said Mama. "Any time you come, you can have all the carrots you want."

Suddenly, Lana heard her mother calling from far away.

"Goodness, I forgot about my parents. They will be worried. I must go."

The children were sad to see their new friend go.

"I will help you whenever you need me," called Lana as she leaped over the wall and headed across the grassland.

"OK," cried the children. "Bye! Bye!" they all called.

They watched Lana disappear into the night. Then they picked up several sticks and went into the house to cook dinner. Papa was glad to see them home safely.

"Where were you?" Lana's mother scolded.

"Oh, I was just eating and I had some carrots."

Lana's mother looked at her daughter queerly. She didn't know what carrots were and she wasn't going to ask.

"Well, from now on you eat close to us so we can watch you," her mother instructed.

"Yes, Mother," Lana replied but she knew she would visit her friends again and get some more of those delicious carrots.

THE END

55

LESTER SAVES THE DAY

"Quack! Quack! Quack!" called Lester, as he waddled to the edge of the lake and entered the water.

But none of the geese or ducks paid any attention. Poor Lester was an orphaned duck. His parents had been shot by hunters a month ago and Little Lester was simply rejected by the other birds who lived on Dam Lake. It was called Dam Lake because it was formed after a huge dam had been constructed many years ago.

Dam Lake was beautiful. Its deep water was pure and clear and it was completely surrounded by tall pine trees. In the winter, large snowflakes fell and made everything white. Dam Lake was a wonderful place to live and Lester loved it.

Ranger Joe realized Lester was an orphan and he often fed him bread and other treats. Unfortunately, this only made the other birds jealous and more determined not to associate with Lester. When Lester approached any of the other little ducks, their mothers would shoo him away and peck at his tail. Lester always fled in fright. But there was no one to nurse his hurt feelings.

So Lester just played by himself except when Ranger Joe came on his horse. Then Lester would hurry out of the water and quack a greeting to his friend. Lester ate right out of Ranger Joe's hand and Ranger Joe would pet him gently.

"Oh my, you are getting to be such a big duck," Ranger Joe would tease.

That made little Lester feel so proud. But he always felt a little sad when his friend got on his horse and rode away to patrol the forest. But Lester knew he would come back and that made him feel better. Then he would smile and go back into the water and have a nice swim.

Lester's favorite place to swim was at the base of the huge dam. Water always spilled out of the big pipes and made a pleasant gurgling sound. Lester liked to swim under the falling water and give himself a shower. Then he would swim near the shore and find lots of tender shoots to eat.

Most of the birds avoided the base of the dam when Lester was there. They swam somewhere else. The lake was so big that there were plenty of other places for them to swim.

One sunny afternoon, as Lester swam near the base of the dam, he noticed a crack in the wall. This is strange, Lester thought. It was kind of a little crack but it wasn't there before, Lester was sure.

The next day, Lester went to look at the crack again. It was still there alright. But it looked a little bigger.

"Oh well, I guess it's OK," Lester said out loud.

Two days later, Lester went to look again. "It's definitely getting bigger," he said. He wondered why this crack was growing. But he had no one to ask so he just kept it inside. But every day Lester came to look at the crack. And little by little it got longer and longer.

Then one day Lester saw water trickling from the crack.

"My goodness," he exclaimed. "The water is coming right through the wall!"

Lester tilted his head way back and looked to the top of the dam. If there is water all the way to the top and it comes through the wall, it will drown Dam Lake and all the birds and their nests and their babies, Lester reasoned. Now he was very concerned.

The next day he came back. Just as he feared! The crack was much bigger and water was coming through much faster. "The dam will break!" Lester exclaimed.

He turned and swam as fast as his little feet could paddle.

"Quack! Quack!" he called loudly. "The dam is breaking! The dam is breaking!"

The other birds looked in his direction but paid no attention at first. Then a few became concerned as Lester continued to dash about in great alarm.

Ranger Joe had just rode up and saw Lester swimming as fast as he could, away from the dam. He heard Lester's excited quacks.

What could have frightened Lester like that? he wondered.

Then one of the elder ducks swam to the dam to have a look. He inspected the wall but he saw no danger. Just as he was about to turn away, he saw water trickling through a crack. The duck gasped in horror, then turned and fled.

"He's right! The dam is breaking! Swim for your lives!" he quacked loudly.

With that, all the birds started to flee, heading towards the other end of the lake where it might be safer. All were quacking and honking.

When Ranger Joe saw this, he knew something was wrong. He pointed his horse toward the dam and galloped off. He stopped abruptly near the water's edge and took out his binoculars. He studied the wall carefully. Then he saw the crack.

"Oh, my gosh!" he cried.

Ranger Joe quickly pulled out his cell phone and reported the problem to Ranger Headquarters. Then he galloped his horse all around the lake, warning campers and hikers to flee for their lives.

Soon crews of men, risking their lives, and many trucks and equipment descended upon the dam. After working all day and through the night, the dam was fixed.

Ranger Joe rode to the far end of the lake where all the birds huddled together on the shore. All except Lester who was hiding behind a tree all by himself and very frightened. When he heard Ranger Joe's horse, he peeked out. There was Ranger Joe. Lester felt very relieved.

Lester rushed out to meet his friend, quacking loudly, "The dam is breaking!" This set all the ducks and geese to quack and honk in terror. They cowered together.

Ranger Joe picked Lester up and held him in the palm of his hand.

"The dam is all fixed, little fella. You and your friends can all go back to your homes."

He smiled warmly at Lester. Then he walked to the edge of the water and set Lester down gently in the shallow water.

My friend wouldn't put me in the water unless it was safe, Lester thought. The other birds watched in awe.

Lester swam around in a circle a few times. Nothing bad happened.

"Hey," he called to all the birds, "it's OK. The dam must be fixed."

At first, the birds refused to move. Then the elder waddled forward and slowly entered the water. After making a few circles, he called, "Everything seems to be alright."

Then all the birds cautiously entered the water. The elder duck opened one of his wings and swam up to Lester. Lester thought the duck was going to shoo him away and was prepared to get away fast if that was the case. But the elder duck smiled and put his wing around the little duck.

"You were very brave to warn us," he said tenderly. Lester snuggled against him and smiled.

"Yes!" cried the other birds. "Thank you!"

Then all the little ducks and goslings swam up to Lester and wanted to be friends. Even pretty Aleda swam up to Lester and fluttered about.

I wonder if she likes me, Lester asked himself in disbelief.

Ranger Joe looked on happily as all the birds swam around Lester, quacking and honking and making such a noise. He watched as they all swam back towards their homes.

And he noticed, with a wink, that the last two little ducks were Lester and Aleda, swimming very slowly, side by side.

THE END

HUMPHREY THE BABY HORSE

Humphrey was a six-month-old colt who lived on a farm with his parents. He loved to frisk about in the pasture, jumping, kicking and running as fast as he could.

Humphrey's mother, Marey, used to be a show horse and was still very pretty. His father, Harold, used to be a race horse. He even won a race once. But now Harold and Marey were retired and had been sold to Happy Farms. Mr. and Mrs. Lacey owned Happy Farms. They loved to buy race horses and show horses whose careers were over and give them a happy retirement home on their farm.

The Laceys loved animals so much that they also had two dogs, two cats, two rabbits and two other horses. Once they had a mule but she died at an old age. The Laceys were very happy when Humphrey was born. All of the animals liked Humphrey and they all got along together very well.

The Laceys had two children, Billie, 13, and Holly, 11. They loved animals, too, and helped feed and care for them. They would bring treats like carrots and apples for the horses and sometimes lumps of sugar. When the horses saw Billie and Holly coming towards the fence, they knew there were treats and they all headed to meet them to be fed and petted.

At first Humphrey was too shy to put his head through the fence rails. He stayed close to his mother. He heard the children laughing and talking and saw them holding out their hands. The other horses went right up and ate what the children offered, even Humphrey's parents. And they let the children pet them, too. Finally, Humphrey could stand it no longer. He had to taste what the children offered.

"Come on! Come on!" called the children to Humphrey.

"Go ahead," Marey coaxed.

Cautiously, Humphrey moved forward, staying as close to his mother as he could. He stretched his neck and sniffed the carrots and apples. First he took a bite of carrot and quickly pulled his head back.

"Ummm, this is good," Humphrey told his mother as he chomped.

Marey smiled.

Humphrey moved forward and took a whole apple right out of Billie's outstretched hand. Then he pulled back before either of the children could pet him.

"Ummm, this is really good," said Humphrey. The apple was sweet and juicy.

Soon all the treats were gone. The children left and the horses turned away.

"Darn!" said Humphrey to his mother. "Next time I am going to get to the fence first and get more of those treats."

Then he raced to the middle of the pasture and challenged his father to a race around the field. Marey smiled. Seeing her son happy made her feel good.

The next time Billie and Holly came to the fence, Humphrey raced to meet them. He was there before any of the other horses and got the first apple and carrot. While he ate, Billie and Holly laughed and petted his neck and head. He liked that. He quickly ate his treats but before he could get more, the other horses came and pushed him away. Each horse got a treat, Billie and Holly made sure of that, right from the refrigerator so they were nice and cool.

One night the horses had been left out to sleep under the stars. They were all sound asleep when suddenly a wind rose up. It was a cool wind. Then it began to rain and pour. The horses huddled together but soon they were all cold and wet. After a time, the rain stopped. Humphrey felt miserable. He was not happy and moved close to his mother for warmth.

In the morning, Billie and Holly came running out, wearing rubber boots to get through the wet grass and mud. They opened the barn door and the horses hurried in. It was no fun being out in that nasty weather.

Each horse had a stall with straw on the floor and hay to eat in the bin. The children brought towels and rubbed each horse until it was fairly dry.

"Oh, poor horses. You got so wet," the children sympathized.

The horses munched hay and enjoyed their rubbings.

When the children came to Humphrey and Marey, Humphrey tried to hide behind his mother.

"Come on, Humphrey, let us dry you. Then you will feel better," they chided.

Finally, they caught him and began rubbing him briskly with their towels. It felt nice, Humphrey thought. He was too tired to resist anymore, anyway. Humphrey just didn't feel well. Then he sneezed. And sneezed again.

"I hope Humphrey isn't catching a cold," said Holly. "It's not good for horses to catch colds."

Billie agreed.

Humphrey had no energy. He never felt this way before. He didn't like it. Marey nuzzled him gently. She knew he wasn't his usual playful self. But that was all she could do for her little son. Humphrey felt like lying down, so he did. The straw felt soft and dry and soon Humphrey dozed off.

In the afternoon, Humphrey was not better. He lay with his legs folded under him and could hardly hold his head up. The children came and put a blanket around Humphrey and offered him an apple. But poor Humphrey had no appetite, not even for a delicious, red apple. He didn't even eat any hay or oats.

The children were concerned. It was not normal for a horse not to eat, especially an apple or oats.

"Maybe we should tell mom," Billie suggested.

"Yes," replied Holly.

They hurried to the house. It was still a gray, chilly day.

Soon the children hurried from the house, followed by Mr. and Mrs. Lacey. They all went into the Humphrey's stall. Marey was glad to see them and nickered. She knew they would help her baby.

Mrs. Lacey knelt down and hugged Humphrey's neck. He was too weak to resist. "What's wrong, baby?" she asked in a soothing voice.

Mr. Lacey looked at Humphrey with an experienced eye. He ran his hands over the colt's body.

"He feels like he has a little temperature," he said.

"Should we call Dr. Brown?" Mrs. Lacey asked.

"I think so. Keep his blanket on and I'll call him," Mr. Lacey said.

The children looked on anxiously. They knew that a baby horse could get pneumonia and become very sick, maybe even die.

Mr. Lacey left them with Humphrey. He called Dr. Brown and returned to the barn. They all watched and waited quietly. Mrs. Lacey still had her arms around Humphrey's neck.

In thirty minutes, Dr. Brown's car was heard and he came into the barn, carrying his black leather bag. The Laceys were glad to see him.

"Hello," they called in unison.

"Hello," smiled Dr. Brown.

He knelt down in the straw and looked Humphrey over. Then he took Humphrey's temperature. "What's wrong, little fella? Not feeling well?" the doctor asked.

"Hmmm," said the doctor, as he read the thermometer. "It's up a little but not too bad." Everyone felt relieved.

Then Dr. Brown gave Humphrey a shot in his rump and forced some medicine down his throat. At first Humphrey tried to pull his head away but Mrs. Lacey held him tightly. Once he tasted the medicine, it wasn't too bad. In fact it tasted syrupy.

"Give him two ounces at five and nine," Dr. Brown ordered. "He should sleep OK and be better in the morning. I think he will be OK," Dr. Brown smiled.

Everyone walked out of the barn with Dr. Brown. They watched until his car was out of sight. Then they went into the house. There was nothing more to do but let the medicine and nature take their course.

Mr. and Mrs. Lacey gave Humphrey his medicine promptly, as the children watched. By evening, Humphrey was standing up. He ate some oats, a little hay and a piece of apple. The Laceys were pleased to see him feeling better. So was Marey. She nuzzled little Humphrey and nickered softly.

The next morning, the sun was out. It was going to be a nice day. Billie and Holly hurried from the house to see Humphrey. Mr. Lacey had checked him earlier and was pleased with what he saw. The children could see that Humphrey was better. They let the other horses out of the barn, even Marey. But not Humphrey, even though he wanted to go out.

Mrs. Lacey told the children to keep Humphrey in his stall for the morning. "If it remained a pleasant day, he could go out in the afternoon," she told them.

Humphrey whinnied for his mother. He stood at the gate to his stall and watched the horses hurry out, even his mom. He felt sad at being left behind.

"Don't worry, Humphrey, we'll stay with you," the children consoled. Then they gave him an apple, a carrot and a sugar lump and brushed and curried him from head to foot.

By mid-day the sun still shone warm in the sky. It was a perfect day so it was decided to let him out. The children took off his blanket and opened the gate. Humphrey dashed out and through the open barn door. As soon as he was outside, he jumped and kicked and raced to his mother. The warm sun felt good on his coat.

The Laceys stood at the fence and watched. They laughed as Humphrey raced about, enjoying his freedom.

"He certainly is well," said Mrs. Lacey.

"Yes," everyone replied happily.

And Humphrey lived happily ever after on Happy Farms. When he was almost two years old, he let Billie and Holly ride on his back. He had a fine saddle and bridle and loved to give the children fast rides over the trails and fields.

He grew up to be a fine horse and never tired of his treats of apples and carrots and especially sugar lumps. His parents were very proud of him.

THE END

TERI THE TORTOISE

Teri the Tortoise lived in a large pond in a tropical climate. The pond was surrounded by large trees and plants of all kinds. A stream flowed into one side of the pond and another flowed out on the other side. So there was always a gentle flow of water coming in and out of Teri's pond.

In the middle of the pond was a large flat rock and Teri climbed on it every day and sunned himself. When he was hungry or thirsty, he slid into the water and cooled himself and took a nice drink. Then he would eat several tasty mosquitoes and climb back on his rock and rest.

Teri had several friends who lived in the pond, also. There was Eli, Snorky and Gumbo. They were all brightly-colored fish who lived peacefully in the cool clear water of the pond. Teri and the fish played together every day. They swam about and chased each other and had a swell time.

And every day Feline the tiger and her two cubs came down for a drink. Teri let the two cubs play with him. They would poke him with their paws while Teri was safely hidden in his shell. Feline would smile at their antics. It made her happy to see her cubs having fun and exploring.

Then there was Shana the deer with her baby, Debbie. They came to drink every day, also. Debbie liked to watch the fish jump and splash when she came for her drink. Her mother always warned her not to get too distracted because Feline might come. Then they would have to run away and come back later.

"I will be careful, mother" Debbie promised.

Teri and his friends liked to see all the animals come to the pond for a drink. Feline even jumped into the pond to cool off if she was particularly hot. But Feline never bothered Teri or the fish. Most tigers don't eat fish.

Sometimes Teri would slowly walk out of the pond and take a look around. There wasn't much to see but he liked to roam around the edge of the pond and sniff the greens and the wild flowers. After a while, he would walk back and ease himself into the cool water and swim about. The fish always asked him what he saw. They wished they could go on the land like Teri. But they knew they couldn't.

One day when Teri was having an excursion on the land, he came upon Debbie. She was hiding in the brush. She was trembling and big tears ran down her cheeks.

"What's wrong, Debbie?" Teri asked.

"Oh, I lost my mother. I don't know where she is. I am afraid. Can you help me?" she asked.

"I will try," said Teri. "Let me climb up on your back so I can see better."

With that, Teri climbed up on Debbie's back. It wasn't easy since Teri's legs were so short. But he finally made it.

"Now, stand up so I can see better. I will watch out for Feline," he added.

Suddenly Feline jumped out of the brush. Debbie leaped back and froze. "I have lost my cubs," Feline cried.

"Oh, that's too bad," Teri responded. "Debbie is lost, too. Perhaps we can all look together."

Debbie wasn't too sure of walking about with Feline the tiger after everything her mother had told her about tigers.

"It's OK," Teri assured her. So the three set out. Soon there was a noise in the brush and Teri saw Shana starting to run. Shana had sensed Feline's presence and fled from her hiding place.

"Wait!" called Teri.

"Mother!" cried Debbie.

Shana stopped immediately. She looked about cautiously. She could barely see Teri now.

"It's OK, Shana," Teri called. "Debbie and I came to find you and we met Feline. She has lost her cubs."

Shana couldn't believe her ears. A tiger walking with a deer! Then she composed herself. "I just passed them. They are hiding in the hollow of the great tree near the clearing."

"I know that tree," Feline exclaimed. And she dashed off, right past Shana.

Shana dashed up to Debbie and licked her face all over. Debbie was so happy to see her mother and she rubbed her face against her neck. When the two had reacquainted themselves, Shana said to Debbie, "Come, we must go."

"Can you take me back to the pond?" Teri asked. "It's too hard to walk through this underbrush."

"Certainly we can," Shana said. And they turned back to the pond, with Teri firmly on Debbie's back.

When they reached the pond, Debbie walked into the water up to her belly and Teri slid off her back and into the water with a splash.

Then Shana and Debbie turned and disappeared into the jungle. Teri's friends immediately swam up. "Gosh, Teri," Eli asked, "where did you go for so long?"

And Teri told them all about how Debbie had lost her mom and Feline had lost her cubs and how they found them. The fish listened with great interest.

"You are lucky," Snorky said. "You get to go out of the water and have lots of fun and excitement. I wish I could do that."

"Well, be happy that you are a fish and can swim with ease and you don't have to worry about getting lost," Teri counseled.

"I guess you are right," Snorky replied.

Then he shouted, "Let's race around the pond three times. The one who is first wins a ride on Teri's back."

And off they raced. They were glad they lived in such a nice pond.

THE END

THE KNIGHT AND THE FISH

By the time the knight reached the Lake of the Dragon, he was tired, very tired. He even felt weary! For he had traveled a great distance. He climbed down from his tired but faithful horse, El Esperanzo, and sat by the bank of the lake. It was late afternoon and the sun was low in the sky, as it usually is at this time of day.

"Whew!" he sighed. "I am tired!"

He laid his lance and his sword on the grass. Then he pulled off his silver helmet and then unbuckled his heavy breast plate, laying them beside him on the grass. Then he pulled off his leather boots and laid them next to his armor. Finally he lowered his tired, hot feet into the cool water of the lake.

"AHHH!" he sighed, as he closed his eyes and felt his body relaxing. This feels good, he thought.

After a moment, he opened his eyes and looked about. This was truly the Lake of the Dragon. Of that he was sure. But there was no dragon in sight. Not yet, anyway.

King Mort had heard many complaints from the people of the area. This dragon was frightening them with his great hulk and fiery breath. So he selected Louie to handle the matter.

Now Louie was not really a knight. Not yet, anyway! He needed one more great deed to become a full knight and earn the title of "Sir." After this adventure, he would be Sir Louie, Knight of the Realm of King Mort. His spirits rose at the thought.

But why couldn't he have been picked to rescue a damsel? That would have been more to his liking and was ever so more romantic than catching a dragon. Poor me, he thought. "Alas!"

At this very moment, Dragon Millie poked her head above the water from the middle of the lake. She was taking her afternoon swim and spied Louie, soon to be Sir Louie, sitting on the bank.

"Hmmm! I wonder who this can be?" she thought. She submerged herself and paddled towards the stranger who had his feet in her lake. Dragons are very good swimmers!

When she was near the bank, she raised her head from the water, keeping her great bulk hidden. She gave Louie a terrible fright, I can tell you. His thoughts were far away, back at the castle where there was dancing, music and fine food.

Seeing only this strange head sticking out of the water, Louie called, "Oh! Who are you?"

"I?" asked Millie. "Why I am just a fish, taking my afternoon swim. Who are you?"

"I am Louie, soon to be Sir Louie, a knight of King Mort, come to tame a dragon who is frightening the people," Louie announced with authority.

"Oh," answered Millie. "I know her. She doesn't really mean to frighten the

people. They come to the lake and when they see her they just run away, screaming that a dragon is loose! They don't even try to be friendly," poor Millie sighed."

Louie put his hand to his mouth. "Oh, my! If that's the case, I can't tame
the beast and I have failed in my mission. Now I won't be Sir Louie or a full
knight and King Mort will be furious!" Louie was upset and in a fret. He put his
head in his hands and began to weep.

Millie felt sorry for poor Louie. Then she replied, "Why don't you go to the
village and tell the people that the dragon wants to be friends? Then they will tell
the king that you have tamed me, I mean the dragon, and the king will be
pleased as anything. You may even get a medal!"

Louie stopped crying and lifted his head. He smiled. "Yes, that is an
excellent idea." He clapped his hands together with joy. "When can I tell the
people to meet the dragon?"

"Oh, tell them to come tomorrow at ten and tell them to bring those lovely
scones they bake. You can smell them cooking for miles. They smell delicious."
Millie smiled with anticipation.

Louie pulled on his boots and jumped to his feet. He grabbed up his
belongings and mounted El Esperanzo. "I shall go immediately. Thank you!
Thank you!" he called as he galloped away, with his armor banging loudly.

Millie smiled and turned to continue her swim.

Louie arrived at the village in a state of great excitement. He called
everyone out and gave them the message that Millie had imparted to him.

"Who told you this?" one wary villager asked.

"Why a fish in the Lake of the Dragon," Louie answered naively.

"A FISH!" they all called, and they laughed mightily. Louie was
embarrassed.

"Yes," answered Louie meekly. Then he regained his confidence and
challenged them - "If you don't believe me, come to the lake in the morning. At
ten!"

"And bring plenty of scones?" one scoffed. "Yes, that's what the fish said,"
they all laughed.

Then the Lord Mayor spoke: "King Mort wouldn't send Sir Louie to us
unless he was an honest man." Everyone nodded and grunted in agreement. "So
let's do as he suggests. If he is not truthful, I will personally lead a delegation to
the king and this man will be punished."

Everyone thought for a moment and then they all shouted in agreement.
Then the Lord Mayor said, "Tomorrow we will go to the lake and see if the
dragon is indeed there. Now let's go to our homes and bake some scones."

Louie had a fretful night, I can tell you. If the fish was fooling him, he would
be in a terrible situation. He would be banned from the knighthood forever!

The next morning, before ten, Louie led the villagers, laden with their
scones, to the lake. They gathered round the bank and stared into the water.
Suddenly, Millie lifted her head from the water. "Good morning," she called,
with a smile.

The villagers were startled for a moment. "That's no dragon," the Lord Mayor cried. "That's a fish!"

"Yes! That's a fish!" they all cried, angrily. Louie's knees went weak.

"Oh," said Millie. "Wait, I will show you."

Millie began to wade to shore. As she reached the shallow water, her enormous body emerged. The villagers shrank back in horror, almost frozen in place. Even Louie was frightened and he was a knight! Well, almost!

Soon Millie was completely out of the water and reclined on the grassy bank, being careful not to crush anyone. No one spoke. It was very quiet. Then little Lucy came forward with her little basket of scones, "I made some scones. Would you like one?" she asked nervously.

"I would love one," Millie answered in her daintiest voice and with a broad smile. "They look and smell delicious!"

She leaned forward and daintily took a scone from little Lucy's outstretched hand. "Oh, my! They are more delicious than I imagined," she exclaimed. "May I have another?"

Lucy smiled warmly and held out another scone. Then all the villagers crowded closer, 'Try one of mine," this one called. "Mine, too," another offered. Soon all the villagers were seated on the grass with their scones before them and all were eating and chatting like old friends. Louie bravely stood leaning against Millie's side and munched on scones. Why he was as brave as any knight in the realm, he thought. Even braver!

They asked Millie many questions, like how long have you been a dragon and how long have you lived in the lake? Millie answered all of their questions patiently, enjoying every minute. She realized how lonely she had been and how nice it was to have so many friends.

When everyone was finished eating, they hesitantly rose to leave. "Can we come back?" little Lucy asked.

"Why of course," answered Millie. "And I will give all the children a ride on my back, all the way to the other side of the lake."

The children squealed with excitement and the parents smiled at their children's happiness. Yes, it has been a fine morning! The villagers bid their good-byes to Millie and went home feeling safe and happy.

The Lord Mayor said to Louie, "I shall personally lead a delegation to the king and tell him of what you have done."

Louie's chest swelled with pride. "Sir Louie" it would surely be. King Mort would reward him for his fine service and his fellow knights would admire him.

At the fork in the road, Louie bid good-bye to the villagers and turned towards the castle. He might get there before night, if he hurried. He was anxious to make a full report to the king and his fellow knights. There would be feasting tonight!

"Ah! It was good to be a knight!" he said to himself.

THE END

LIONEL THE LION CUB

Did you know that long ago in a land so far away, there lived a lion cub, Lionel was his name. Lionel lived in a cozy den with his mother Leona and his sister Simbrina.

When Leona went to hunt for food, Lionel and Simbrina stayed home and played and wrestled, like all lion cubs. Before Leona left, she always reminded her cubs to stay close to the den and never wander off.

"Yes, mother," they would reply, like good children.

But one day when Simbrina was napping, Lionel began to explore outside the den. He scampered after a butterfly. Then he came upon a large land turtle. The turtle hid in its shell when Lionel approached. Lionel pawed the turtle's hard shell and snarled bravely. But he could do nothing with the big, old turtle and soon he got bored. So he continued his excursion.

Soon he came upon a mother possum with her brood of six little ones. They all ran up a tree as soon as their mother called, "LION!" Lionel could not understand why they ran away. He wanted to play. He wasn't going to hurt them.

So he continued on, a little disappointed. Then he came upon a baby gnu who was hiding in the grass. Lionel scampered around the little gnu, sniffing and touching it gently with his paw. The gnu lay very still but was shaking a little.

"What's your name?" asked Lionel.

"Newton," answered the baby.

"My name is Lionel. I am a lion. Do you want to play?"

Then he gave a fierce snarl.

Newton became more frightened and continued to shake.

"Oh," asked Lionel, "Did I frighten you? I am sorry. I won't snarl anymore."

Newton believed Lionel and smiled. He felt better now. Then he got up and began to frisk about. He put his head down and charged at Lionel who quickly got out of the way.

As soon as he got a chance, Lionel jumped on Newton's back and gave him a nip on his shoulder. Newton bucked and Lionel fell off - PLOP! The two began romping about, chasing each other and laughing and giggling.

Suddenly Newton's mother came. When she saw Lionel, she became frightened and charged, sending Lionel reeling. Poor Lionel was confused but instinctively got out of the way. Then the mother gnu charged again and sent Lionel racing back home.

He ran into the cozy den, panting and all out of breath, tumbling into his sister who had been asleep.

"What's the matter?" she asked, suspiciously.

Lionel told Simbrina about his adventures and all about his new friend

Newton.

"You disobeyed mother and went into the jungle," Simbrina scolded.

"Well, I only went a little way," Lionel offered, apologetically. "It wasn't far!"

Simbrina was not appeased. "You'd better not do that again or I will tell mother," she warned.

Lionel put his head down and looked away, avoiding the cold stare of his sister.

Meanwhile, Newton's mother was scolding him. "That was a lion. Didn't I tell you never to go near a lion?"

"Yes, mother," Newton answered, sheepishly.

"You must never, never play with that lion again," she warned.

"Yes, mother," Newton answered. He wanted to ask why but decided not to.

The next day, as soon as Leona went out to hunt, Lionel snuck away while Simbrina was exploring an ant hill. He soon found his friend Newton, hiding in the grass.

When they saw each other they immediately began frisking about and laughing. They were glad to see each other. They had great fun playing in the jungle and exploring. When it was time to go, Lionel told Newton he would come back tomorrow.

"OK," replied Newton but he was a little sad to see his friend leave.

So Lionel and Newton played together almost every day. Each was growing swiftly, as all jungle animals do. But one day Leona took Lionel and Simbrina off to teach them to hunt. Newton's mother took him out to a large grassy plain where they joined a great herd of gnus. Lionel and Newton never saw each other again. Well, not for a long time, anyway.

One day, months later when Lionel and Newton had grown up, Lionel was walking along the edge of the great grassy plain. Suddenly he heard a great commotion. A pack of hyenas was chasing a gnu. The gnu was running as fast as it could but the hyenas were gaining.

Why, that's Newton, Lionel remembered. Those hyenas are trying to catch him.

With a mighty roar, Lionel bolted forward, running after the hyenas. His long, powerful strides had him quickly gaining on the pack.

Newton ran this way and that, with the hyenas right on his heels. Lionel could see Newton was tiring.

When Newton could no longer run, he spun around to face his pursuers, standing with his back against a large tree. He would have to fight! He lowered his head, ready to butt the hyenas with his sharp horns. But truly, he was no match for so many.

The hyenas approached cautiously, snarling. They knew those sharp horns could hurt them if they weren't careful. They slowly advanced, showing their razor-sharp teeth and waiting for the opportunity to charge for the kill.

Suddenly Lionel jumped right into the middle of the pack. His mighty roar surprised and frightened the hyenas and even Newton. They froze in fear.

Lionel gave the closest one such a blow with his paw that it went flying through the air. When it landed on the ground with a thud and a yelp, it got up and ran away.

The next one he gave a vicious bite to its hind quarter and sent it yelping away in pain. All the time Lionel was snarling and growling. The noise spread through the jungle!

Then Newton charged and butted a hyena before it had a chance to dodge. It too yelped in pain and ran off. The rest of the pack quickly followed. They had enough.

"Lionel!" cried Newton, excitedly.

"Newton, my old friend," exclaimed Lionel.

The two rubbed noses and were glad to see each other. Soon they were running about and playing, just as they did when they were younger. Well, after all, they were not even two years old!

The other gnus and lions looked on in surprise at seeing a lion and gnu romping about. Leona and Newton's mother could not believe their eyes. What kind of children did we raise, they wondered.

The hyenas ran off and licked their wounds. And from then on, they never tried to catch Newton again. They learned their lesson.

And Lionel and Newton remained fast friends for the rest of their lives. And when Newton had a son, he named it Lionel. And Lionel named one of his sons Newton. And those two cubs played together just like their fathers did.

THE END

STOOFA THE BABY CAMEL

The caravan of six camels and four men moved slowly across the desert. The camels each carried a large load but seemed to have no difficulty managing.

This was the monthly trek from Mumba to Loozi, a distance of two hundred miles. The camels carried many items which would be sold and traded at Loozi. Then many goods from Loozi would be brought back to Mumba. So each town traded its goods with the other.

The journey took ten days with four oasis stops for rest and water. Much of the traveling was done at night to avoid the heat of the day. At night the desert is cool and a full moon gives plenty of light.

Oh, yes, there was one baby camel named Stoofa. His mother was Lulu. She was nice and she had made this journey for several years. She was used to it but lately it seemed more difficult.

Am I getting old, she wondered.

Sometimes Stoofa wondered if his mother's load was too heavy and he wished he could carry something. But he was told he was too young, yet.

"When I get big, I will carry all of your goods, mother," Stoofa would tell her. "Then you can just walk along like I do. It will be easy!"

"Yes, dear," his mother would answer, pleased with her son's concern.

Stoofa loved the oasis. There was always cool water to drink, all he wanted. And there were usually some fresh dates for a treat.

After dinner, everyone lay down around a nice fire and the men took out their musical instruments and played and sang. Everyone had a fine time!

When they arrived at Mumba, the camels were led to a market place and all of the goods were unloaded and spread out on carpets. Then people came to see the goods from Loozi and bought what they needed.

When all the items were sold, the men bought goods that were needed in Loozi and loaded them onto the camels and journeyed back across the desert.

Mumba was a bigger village than Loozi and Stoofa was a little afraid of so many people so he stayed close to his mother. For two days, the camels just rested until it was time to load up and return home.

On this occasion, the men seemed pleased with the trading that had taken place and were eager to pack up and start for home to see their wives and children.

Before loading, Josef, one of the camel drivers, was talking to bin Alla.

"I am concerned with Lulu. I think the heavy load is getting too much for her."

"Why don't you give some to Stoofa?" bin Alla suggested.

"I was thinking of that, old friend," Josef replied. "I am glad you are of the same opinion!"

"Yes, I think Stoofa is big enough to carry some things."

So Josef made a nice bundle and strapped it on Stoofa's back. OH, Stoofa was so proud!

"Look, mother," Stoofa called. "See the large bundle I shall carry. Now you will have an easy time of walking home!"

"I see," Lulu answered. "I am very proud of you, my son, and thank you."

Stoofa walked up and down in front of the other camels, showing them his heavy load, which was really not so heavy. The camels just looked but showed no emotion. You know how camels are!

Then it was time to start back. The camels lined up and filed out of Mumba as the villagers all took notice.

"Good-bye!" they called. "See you next month!"

The drivers waved back and smiled.

"Good-bye! See you next month," they called.

Stoofa strutted along with his head up and chest out. I bet they are noticing me, he thought.

And soon they were out of the village and into the desert, facing the long journey home. The excitement was gone now and Stoofa became aware that he had to carry his not-so-heavy load all the way back to Loozi. But he did not complain or show his mother that he was having any trouble carrying his bundle.

He was very glad to get to the first oasis and have his bundle removed. "Wow! That feels good!" he told his mother. She smiled in agreement.

And the days went by and soon the outline of Loozi could be seen in the distance! Spirits rose and the pace picked up. As they got closer, the people of Loozi came out to greet the men.

Once again, Stoofa lifted his head and strutted to show all the villagers how easily he carried his not-so-large bundle. Oh, they noticed right away and nodded with approval.

It was too late to display any of the goods from Mumba so the camels were just unloaded and placed in their stalls with some nice hay and oats to eat. There would be plenty of time tomorrow to sell what was purchased in Mumba.

Stoofa snuggled right up to his mother as they lay on their soft straw. He was proud of his work and of making his mother's work easier. Now they had a long rest before starting back. Stoofa was glad for that.

And tonight, all the camels would sleep well in the cool desert air. Their long journey had tired all of them and it was good to be home.

Maybe I shall have an even bigger bundle when we go to Mumba, Stoofa thought. Oh, his mother would have an easier trip then.

A little smile came across his face as he drifted off to a fine, deep sleep, looking forward to tomorrow and seeing the little boy who took care of him who always brought his favorite treat - fried dates!

THE END

72

TUFFY THE PUMA

The first snow of winter had fallen on most of Montana and a three-inch blanket covered the ground at Wiley Farm. The air was clear and crisp and the sky was cloudless. Fifteen-year-old Jeeter and his younger sister Sara walked quietly together. They were warmly dressed with sweaters, jackets, scarves, hats and gloves but they could still feel the cold. Their boots made two paths across the leveled farm land. Looking back, the children could see the curves their footprints had made in the snow, not the straight line they imagined. In the distance was the farm house. It seemed far away.

"Doesn't it look weird?" Sara asked softly. "It seems like we are walking in a straight line but look at our tracks."

Jeeter agreed. They continued to walk. Each carried a .22 rifle. They were hunting. The children often hunted rabbits, squirrels, deer and pheasants in the winter. The meat added to the family diet and was always welcomed.

The Wileys were wheat farmers and managed to eke out a living on their small spread but there was usually little money left after expenses. So a few eggs from their chickens and what was brought home from hunting and fishing was needed.

Jeeter and Sara were good shots, having been taught by their father, Tom, several years ago. They always felt proud when they could bring home some game or fish. That was a high time. Tom Wiley worked in the general store during the winter months as there was not much to do on the farm.

"I hope we get a couple of rabbits," Sara whispered.

"Me, too," answered Jeeter.

They talked softly so as not to scare any game and walked with their rifles at the ready. You only got one shot once a rabbit took off running or a pheasant took to the air. It had to be a good one.

The children looked closely for any tracks in the snow that would tell them if any game was in the area. So far there was not one track nor the sight of anything to eat. The animals often ventured out into the open, searching for bits of wheat that had not been gathered. So far they all seemed to be hiding. Jeeter and Sara had been walking for two hours and they were getting cold.

"Let's go over towards the woods," Jeeter said.

As they approached the tree line, they heard what sounded like a kitten crying. Sometimes a cat had kittens out in the open. The children moved cautiously towards the sound.

As soon as they entered the woods, Jeeter and Sara both jumped backwards. Laying on the ground close by was a puma. If this was her den, she would attack and the children would be in serious trouble. But she didn't move. Jeeter knew something was wrong. Once they regained their composure, they eyed the prone animal with considerable anxiety. But she didn't move.

"Is she dead?" asked Sara.

"I don't know," answered Jeeter, "but we'd better not stay here."

Slowly they began to back away, rifles ready. Suddenly, a baby puma which had been hiding behind his mother scampered away, crying loudly. He startled the children for a moment and they stopped to watch him struggle through the snow. Still the mother did not move.

"She must be dead," Jeeter said softly.

"Oh, the poor baby," sympathized Sara. "He will die. We can't leave him here."

She moved towards the cub, keeping some distance between her and the mother, just in case. Jeeter watched nervously.

As Sara approached the baby, he hissed and the fur on his back stood up. He was afraid and was trying to defend himself.

"It's alright, boy. I won't hurt you," Sara soothed.

The little guy turned and ran and tried to climb a tree. Sara caught up with him and picked him up by the scruff of his neck. He hissed again and swatted at her with his paw.

"Oh, you little tuffy," teased Sara as she grabbed his paw and gave it a shake.

Then he bit her hand. "Ouch!" called Sara, laughing. "His teeth are sharp."

Jeeter couldn't help but grin watching his sister dealing with the cub.

Sara cuddled the cub in her arms and rocked it gently. "There, there," she cooed. "I won't hurt you. Don't be afraid."

At first the cub squirmed and tried to get away but Sara had him fast. She continued to rock and coo and soon the cub lay quietly in her arms.

"I think he likes it," Sara called softly.

"The poor little guy is probably cold and you are warming him," Jeeter speculated.

"Are you cold, little Tuffy?" Sara teased. Then she laughed. "He's purring. You're not so tough, you little softy."

She started to walk towards Jeeter, avoiding the dead mother.

Jeeter reached his hand to pet the cub who instantly hissed and swatted at Jeeter with his paw. But soon he was calm again and let Jeeter pet his head as he lay contented in Sara's arms.

"This little guy must be hungry," Sara said. "We can't let him starve or get eaten by another animal."

Jeeter blinked. What can we do with a puma cub, he wondered.

"Let's bring him home," Sara said. "Mom will know how to take care of him."

"Do you think Mom will get mad if we bring home a cub?" Jeeter asked.

"You know Mom would never let a baby animal die. She will think of something."

Jeeter was hesitant. A baby animal was one thing but a baby puma was something else.

"Come on," Sara insisted. And she started to walk away.

Suddenly a large rabbit bolted from his hiding place right in front of Sara. Instinctively, Jeeter aimed and fired. "I got it!" he shouted. "Maybe Mom won't mind so much now," he added.

They started across the open field, Jeeter with the rabbit tied to his belt and Sara with the cub snuggled in her arms.

Sara talked to the cub as they walked. "Look at you, you little tuffy. All snuggly and cozy. And just a little while ago you were trying to act like a big tiger. Weren't you?"

She kept one hand on his head, caressing it as she talked in a soothing voice. There was no doubt, the little cub was enjoying the attention and seemed content to be carried.

"What shall we call him?" Sara asked.

"Call him Leo," Jeeter replied.

"Leo is a lion's name. You're not a lion, are you, little tuffy?" Then she exclaimed, "That's it! We'll call him Tuffy. That's a perfect name for him."

Sara was pleased with her choice. Jeeter didn't say anything but it was a cute name, he thought.

Soon the trio was at the back door to their house. "I'll go in first with the rabbit," Jeeter said. "Mom will like that."

"OK," replied Sara.

Jeeter opened the door to the kitchen and marched through, holding his rabbit high.

"Hi, Mom, look what I got," he proclaimed.

Eunice Wiley was at the stove and turned when she heard footsteps on the porch.

"Oh, my brave hunters are home and with a fine rabbit," she teased. "Put him outside for now and come and sit. I have cocoa for you."

The children's eyes lit up and they smiled. That sounded so good.

"What's that you have, Sara?" Eunice asked. "Another rabbit?"

"No, Mom. Jeeter and I found this baby and we couldn't let it die."

Eunice peered into her daughter's arms and her jaw dropped. "A puma?" she cried.

"Yes, Mom, and his mother is dead and we couldn't leave it. See how cute he is?"

Sara raised the cub in both her hands. He hissed at Eunice but no cub was going to intimidate her.

"Oh, wait til he gets to know you a little. He is so cute and friendly. We call him Tuffy. Here, hold him and see how affectionate he is."

Before Eunice could say anything, Sara thrust the cub into her mother's hands. Instinctively, Eunice cradled the baby in her arms and soon Tuffy was purring away and thumbing his paw on her chest. His fur was so soft and those dark eyes seemed to be pleading with her, "Let me stay." Eunice melted. Soon she was smiling at little Tuffy and talking to him. Jeeter and Sara knew Tuffy was going to stay.

"Now let's understand something right now," Eunice started, after they were all seated around the table. The children had their cups of cocoa and Eunice had her new baby. "This is a wild animal. We can only keep it for a few months or so then it has to be turned loose. Understood?"

"Oh, yes, Mamma," the children replied happily.

"Now let's see if I can give this baby some milk. He must be hungry."

Eunice rose from the table, placing Tuffy on the floor. Tuffy immediately began sniffing and exploring. "I don't know what your father is going to say," Eunice mumbled.

Then Sara jumped up. "Mom, I still have my baby bottle from my doll set. Will that be OK?"

"Hmm," Eunice responded. "Get it and let's see."

Sara hurried off to her room, with Tuffy right on her heels. Jeeter and Eunice laughed.

"Here it is," Sara called as she entered the kitchen, with Tuffy right behind., batting her ankles instinctively. A little hunter already.

Eunice inspected it. "Wash it up and I'll heat some milk. I hope he takes it."

Soon Eunice was holding her baby in her arms, offering him the bottle of warm milk. At first Tuffy didn't understand and he turned his head away. Eunice was persistent and finally was able to force the nipple into his mouth. Soon Tuffy was holding the bottle tightly with both of his front paws and sucking greedily. Everyone laughed. There was no doubt that Tuffy was cute and hungry.

As soon as the bottle was empty, Tuffy began to cry. "He wants more," Eunice said. The bottle was small so Tuffy drank four before he was finally satisfied.

To everyone's relief, Tom Wiley was excited about having a puma cub for a pet so the whole family became dedicated to the caring of their new baby.

Tuffy took to everyone and was very playful and affectionate. He quickly began stalking the chickens so the coop was securely fenced and Tuffy could only stare and wonder. Otherwise he caused very few problems.

After the first month, Tom relegated Tuffy to the barn. "A puma is not a house pet," he reminded the children. At first, Tuffy cried at being locked in the barn but to everyone's delight, Tuffy instantly became an excellent mouser.

"He's better than four cats," Tom proclaimed proudly.

But Tuffy grew quickly and was soon about seventy-five pounds.

"He's getting awfully big, don't you think, Tom?" Eunice asked one day.

"Yes. He is going to become a danger even if he doesn't mean to," Tom replied in a serious tone.

Eunice shuddered at the thought. "What shall we do?" she asked.

"A little longer," he said sadly. "Then I'll take him in the truck and drive him for fifty miles and turn him loose. Then he is on his own but I think he will be OK."

"We'll have a talk with the children so they can say good-bye," Eunice said.

A month later, Eunice and the children watched tearfully as Tom loaded

Tuffy into the cab of the truck and drove off. Tuffy liked riding in the truck so it was no problem getting him in. Everyone was very sad when Tom came back without Tuffy but no one said anything. Even after a few months, everyone still missed Tuffy. The children hoped he would find his way back but they never saw him.

It was winter again. The first snow came in November and it was cold. The crop was a good one and the price of wheat was higher than last year's so Tom and Eunice were pleased with the results of their labor.

On one December night, everyone was in bed and fast asleep. Suddenly there was a commotion at the chicken coop. Tom jumped into his boots, pulled on his parka, grabbed his rifle and raced for the back door.

The cold air stung his face and quickly made him fully alert. He stopped on the porch and stared at the chicken coop. Soon a large animal bolted and raced for the field. Tom got off a hurried shot with his .30 rifle but he missed.

He turned and went back into the house. Jeeter and Sara were awakened by the commotion and were waiting for their father to come in.

"What was it, Dad?" Jeeter asked.

"I think it was a fox. Maybe we will set a trap tomorrow."

"OK, Dad. I'll help."

"Me, too," called Sara.

The children went back to their rooms and Tom climbed back into bed.

"Was it a fox?" asked Eunice.

"No, it was a large animal. I couldn't see it that well."

Eunice was quiet for a while. Then she asked, "Was it Tuffy?"

"I don't know," Tom answered, almost regretfully. "I hope not."

The next morning, Tom and the children inspected the chicken coop. There were tracks in the snow. Tom knelt to inspect them closely.

"What are those, Dad?" Jeeter asked.

Tom's expression was very serious. "Those are wolf tracks," he answered.

"Gosh, a wolf!" Sara exclaimed. "Will it come back?"

"Probably. It must be hungry to come this close."

After breakfast, Tom got in his truck and drove to work at the general store. Jeeter and Sara bundled up, got their rifles and headed out to hunt.

"Bring back a couple of steaks," Eunice called.

The children laughed and waved good-bye.

After two hours of criss-crossing the wheat field, Jeeter and Sara headed for the woods. There was nothing in the field. Not even a crow called to warn the animals that hunters were on the prowl.

"One more hour and we'll go home," Jeeter said.

"OK. I am really cold," Sara replied.

There were drifts of snow in the woods and some places were hard to get through. The children struggled along and finally agreed to give up for the day. They turned and headed for home.

Suddenly they were right in the path of a snarling wolf. It must have been

77

stalking them for there he was, crouched and poised to attack. His shaggy coat was long and dark and knotted. His sharp, white teeth almost gleamed. It all happened so quickly and he was so close that the children froze in their tracks. They were too frightened to think or react. Their hearts were pounding so hard that they could hardly breathe.

The starving beast was looking right into Jeeter's eyes. He wanted him and was about to spring from his crouch when a wild scream pierced the still air. Something came flying through the air, screaming and snarling and pounced on the unsuspecting wolf. At first everything was a blur to the children. Then they seemed to regain their senses and there was Tuffy, in a battle to the death with the wolf.

The wolf was not about to give up his prey to this intruder and Tuffy was not about to let the wolf harm the children. The wolf's growls and snarls and Tuffy's high-pitched screams shattered the quiet of the woods. The two lunged at each other and then retreated to strike again.

Tuffy slashed at the wolf with his razor-sharp claws which the wolf was clever enough to avoid. Then he would rush at Tuffy, trying to get his fangs into Tuffy's throat.

Tuffy would jump back to avoid the wolf's charge. Then they would circle each other and begin their attacks again, snarling and growling.

By now the children were alert and took aim at the wolf with their rifles. But the clashes were so swift and severe that the children had to continually jump about to avoid getting caught up in the tangle. And neither could get a clear shot at the wolf without the risk of hitting Tuffy.

Suddenly the wolf lunged right for Tuffy's throat and gave a ferocious snarl. As Tuffy leaped back, he slashed at the wolf and caught him right alongside his head. The wolf yelped and tumbled to the ground but before he could recover, Tuffy had him by the throat and pinned him to the ground.

The wolf thrashed wildly and yelped loudly but it was hopeless. Tuffy would not let go and soon the wolf lay lifeless. The children lowered their rifles and watched silently as the victor finished his kill.

Suddenly it was quiet again. Tuffy lifted his head and looked at the children.

"Oh, Tuffy," called Sara, "it's you."

She moved forward but Tuffy quickly backed away. He was crouched, almost as if he were ready to spring. He stared deeply into the faces of the children.

"Tuffy, don't you remember us," Sara asked calmly so as not to alarm him.

Tuffy did not move. His tail flicked nervously.

"Don't go any closer," Jeeter warned.

Jeeter and Sara stood like statues, waiting for Tuffy to make a move, to recognize them and come forward. But after a few moments, he turned and slunk into the woods. Soon he was racing away and quickly out of sight.

They looked at the lifeless body of the wolf and finally realized that they were no longer in danger. They walked home, almost in a daze at the terror they had just experienced.

After they told their parents about what had happened, Sara exclaimed, "It was him, I know it."

"Yes, it was," cried Jeeter.

"We know," Eunice consoled. "But Tuffy has gone back to the wild where he belongs. But in his own way he still loves you."

Then they made a circle and hugged each other.

"If Tuffy didn't still love you, he wouldn't have gotten into a fight. Wolves and cats don't normally fight each other," Tom offered.

"Really, Dad?" Jeeter asked.

"Yes, really."

"Will we ever see Tuffy again?" Sara asked.

"Maybe," Tom answered. "But probably only from a distance. He will never be our pet again."

Jeeter and Sara were saddened to hear those words.

"But you know what I think?" Eunice asked.

"What?" the children responded.

"I think that Tuffy is watching us more often than we think. He still remembers us and he still loves us. So he will watch us even though it's from a distance. And he will protect us whenever he can. That's what I think."

Eunice's last words were said with finality.

"Really, Mom?" the children asked.

"Really!" Eunice answered. "Now, who wants popcorn and a video? Say 'AYE'."

"I do!" Tom and the children answered in unison.

"Tom, the video's on the VCR. I will be back in a minute with the popcorn. Get your seats and comforters and get cozy."

The children scrambled to the sofa and placed their comforters over their laps. Tom set the video in place and settled on the sofa, leaving room for his wife between him and Sara.

The microwave beeped and soon Eunice came sweeping into the room with two large bowls of popcorn. She took her place next to Tom and placed one bowl on his lap and gave the other to Sara and Jeeter. Jeeter and Sara each grabbed a handful of popcorn and began to munch. Tom pressed the PLAY button on the remote and the Wiley family enjoyed a wonderful evening together in the warmth and shelter of their home.

"I hope Tuffy is this comfortable," Sara said.

"With his fur coat and a cozy den, I am sure he is as happy as can be," replied Eunice. "He probably has a wife by now!"

The children smiled warmly at the thought and settled down for an exciting movie.

THE END

THE PRINCE OF WHALES

King Wally waited impatiently for the news of the birth of his first baby. Queen Beulah was overdue. Wally and Beulah were two very large whales who lived in the ocean. It was a large ocean and sometimes a storm would arise and the waves could be 100 feet high. When it was stormy, most the fish went to the bottom of the ocean and waited until the storm was over. But right now, the ocean was calm and serene.

Then King Wally saw Pauly the Porpoise swimming as fast as he could. "This must be the news I am waiting for," said King Wally, hopefully.

Pauly the Porpoise skidded to a halt right in front of King Wally. He bowed to the king. "Well, well, what is it? Do you have any news?" the king asked, anxiously.

Pauly was out of breath but he managed to blurt out the news, "It's a boy! A 250-pound boy!"

King Wally was delighted. "A boy!" he echoed. "Not just a boy but a Prince!" he shouted.

"A Prince!" all the fish exclaimed. Then they all began to cheer which caused a great number of bubbles to rise to the surface of the ocean.

"What shall you call him?" asked Sarah Shark.

"Yes, what is his name?" several other fish asked.

King Wally puffed up his great chest in a very dignified manner and announced, "His name shall be William, after my grandfather."

Everyone became excited. "Hooray for Prince Willy," shouted Sally the Swordfish. And everyone shouted, "Hooray for Prince Willy." Bubble, bubble.

And so the not-so-little baby was known to all as Prince Willy. But when he finally appeared with his mother, he was shy. Then the salmon and the tuna all swam around him, oohing and aahing. And soon the Prince overcame his shyness and he began to play with all the other fish. It was great fun swimming all over the ocean, going fast, twisting and turning and playing tag and hide-and-seek. Prince Willy loved his new friends and the ocean.

When the first storm arose, poor Willy was frightened and he swam to his mother as fast as he could. Queen Beulah calmly led him to the bottom of the ocean where the water was calm. Soon Prince Willy was no longer afraid. His mother explained exactly what a storm was and told him that whenever one arose, he must simply come to the bottom and wait for it to pass. She also warned him about fishermen and warned him to never, never go too close to the shore.

"Why, mother?" Willy asked.

"Because the water by the shore is too shallow and you cannot swim unless the water is deep. You will be stuck on the sand and then the humans will come and eat you."

Willy was very frightened to hear his mother's words. "I won't go too close to the shore," Willy promised.

Sometimes, during a storm, Prince Willy would go to the surface and poke his head above water. He saw the huge waves and he would even get swept away with some of them. It was fun! Prince Willy became a "surfing whale." Then he saw the porpoise and the tuna and some of the other larger fish surfing, too.

"Boy! This is fun," shouted Prince Willy.

One day a storm arose and Prince Willy raced to the surface. He flew out of the water and made a big belly flop which caused a big splash. The waves were high and powerful and Prince Willy let them carry him this way and that.

On one of his flights through the air, Willy saw a strange sight. He had never seen such a thing. "What is that?" called Willy to Pauly the Porpoise.

"That is a sail boat," answered Pauly. "There are humans on it. See?"

Willy jumped into the air for another look at the sailboat. He saw two strange creatures clinging to the mast. They looked frightened.

"They are in trouble," said Pauly. "The waves are too high and their mast is broken and their sail is gone. They shouldn't be out in a storm. They belong in the harbor."

"Where is that?" asked Willy.

"It's about a mile over. See the land on your right?"

Willy could see the land. This was the closest he had ever been to land.

"Maybe I can give them a push to the harbor," Willy called.

"You'd better not," warned Pauly. "It's too dangerous."

Willy saw the sailboat bobbing and dipping. It almost tipped over. The humans would fall into the sea. They cannot swim in this rough water, Willy thought. He headed for the boat. Pauly followed a little distance behind.

When he got to the boat, Willy began to push it as gently as he could. He was pushing it toward the shore. After a while, Willy managed to get the boat into the harbor and close to shore. That is when the humans saw him.

"Look!" shouted one. "This whale has pushed us to safety."

"Yes, I see," answered the other. "Oh, thank you," they cried.

And just as Willy was about to turn back to the sea, he felt something strange. He was touching sand! The only time he touched sand was when he rested on the bottom of the ocean. When he tried to turn away, he could not.

"Look!" cried one of the humans, "He is grounded."

"Oh, no," cried the other. "Let's get to shore and get help." So they started their motor and chugged to shore.

Now Willy understood what his mother had warned him about. "Don't go too close to shore." Now he remembered. And the humans were going to get others so they could eat him. Willy thrashed about as hard as he could but he could not get turned about. In fact, he was sinking deeper into the sand!

"Now they will eat me and I will never see my mother or father or my friends." He began to cry. Whales make large tears when they cry. Soon many humans were coming in small boats.

Then he heard Pauly calling, "Swim! Swim!"

But alas, Willy could not. Now the boats were touching him.

"Get the rope around his tail," he heard someone call. Then he felt something going around his tail and drawing tight. Woe is me, thought Willy.

"That's good. Now we have him," someone called. "Now everyone row as hard as you can."

Willy felt the rope tugging at his tail but he did not move. He lay on his side, pressed tightly against the sand. Then he heard a strange sound. A large boat was coming. There were no oars and no sails but it made a funny sound - PUTT, PUTT! CHUG, CHUG!. RRRRR!

"Tie one end of the rope to me," someone called.

"OK, I've got it," Willy heard someone say.

"Try it now."

"Did he really push your boat to shore?" someone asked.

"He sure did," was the reply.

Then the strange noise from the boat grew louder and louder. Willy felt the rope pulling on his tail. It was beginning to hurt. A large tear rolled down his cheek. "I want my mother," Willy whispered.

The rope pulled harder and harder. Then Willy felt himself begin to move, ever so slowly at first. The humans began to shout, "He's moving! He's moving! Keep going! Don't stop!"

Willy's poor body was being dragged across the sand but the water was getting deeper, Willy could tell that. As soon as it was deep enough, Willy began to swim. Ohh, it felt so good.

"He's swimming! Cut the rope! Cut the rope!"

Willy felt the rope loosen as he raced for the ocean. Pauly was waiting for him. "I knew they would help you if they could," shouted Pauly. "Humans are nice, except for the fishermen."

Willy could hear the humans screaming and shouting. "Hooray! Hooray!"

"They are cheering for you," said Pauly.

Then Willy heard something strange. One of the humans shouted, "Good-bye, Willy, and thanks."

Now Willy and Pauly were out of the harbor and the waves became high, the storm was still blowing.

"Gosh!" said Willy. "They knew my name."

Then he flapped his huge tail out of the water and waved good-bye to the humans just before he and Pauly dove below the surface to where the water was calm.

Willy hurried to his mother and nuzzled her affectionately. His mother was pleased at her son's affection. She didn't know why Willy was so happy to see her and he never told her. From then on he was a very, very good not-so-little whale.

THE END

BEULAH BUNNY'S VERY GOOD IDEA

Gee, it was already December 23 and there was not one bit of snow on Pine Mountain. Not one pine tree had one flake of snow on any of its boughs. The Snow bunnies were very discouraged. Without snow they could not ski, toboggan, snow board, make snowmen, ride their snowmobiles, throw snowballs or anything.

"What fun is winter without snow?" Barry Bunny asked.

"Yes, what fun?" echoed Bobette Bunny.

"Look at Thunder Mountain across the way," observed Barbie Bunny. "Why does it have so much snow and we have none?"

"It's because the snow clouds all went over Thunder Mountain and none came over us," moaned Bertha Bunny.

"Last year we had lots of snow at this time," declared Billy Bunny.

"Tons of snow," added Bobby Bunny.

"What good does last year count?" questioned Benny Bunny. "It's this year that counts. We have to think of something that will make it snow right now!"

"We've thought and thought and talked and talked," cried Bernie Bunny. "We have not come up with one idea that will make it snow."

"Not one," declared Burman Bunny.

"Well, we have to think some more," exclaimed Barry Bunny.

All of the Snow Bunnies sat down and began to think. They thought and thought.

"My brain is tired," whispered Billy Bunny to Bobette Bunny.

"Mine is, too," she whispered back.

"QUIET!" bellowed Benny Bunny. "Who can think with all this talking going on?"

"If we can only get the snow clouds to fly over us," sighed Burman Bunny.

"We know that," said Barbie Bunny, "but how?"

Then a faint voice was heard, "I think I know how."

Everyone turned to see who spoke. Why, it was Beulah Bunny. She was very shy and very quiet. She never had any ideas and no one ever paid any attention to her and didn't invite her to join their games.

"You know how?" laughed Bernie Bunny. Then everyone had a good laugh.

"Beulah never knows how to do anything," Bobby Bunny sneered.

They all turned their backs on poor Beulah. She looked at them sadly and two tears rolled down her cheeks. Then she quietly got up and hopped away. If they don't want to listen to my idea, they don't have to, she said to herself. So she just hopped away and left them all sitting and thinking.

Beulah Bunny hopped all the way to the bottom of Pine Mountain to Ranger Roger's cabin. Ranger Roger was standing on his porch, peering at the sky through his binoculars. He was looking for snow clouds. He knew if there was no snow then all the skiers from the big cities would not come. They would probably go to Thunder Mountain instead. Then the Pine Log Lodge would be closed and all the employees would have to go home with no pay. That would be very sad. Ranger Roger could see all the clouds were hovering over Thunder Mountain.

Ranger Roger lowered his binoculars when he heard Beulah Bunny approaching.

"Hello, Ranger Roger," she called.

"Hello, Beulah," Ranger Roger replied. "What brings you all the way down here?"

"Well, you know we haven't any snow and it's already December 23," she answered, shyly.

"Yes, I know. I am concerned about that."

"Well, I have an idea, sort of," Beulah said, sheepishly, wondering if Ranger Roger would listen or not.

"What is it?" asked Ranger Roger, in a serious tone.

"Well," Beulah went on, "the snow clouds are all blowing over Thunder Mountain." She paused, now she was afraid her idea might sound silly.

"Yes, go on," encouraged Ranger Roger.

"Well, I was thinking if you got into your helicopter, maybe you could fly up and blow the snow clouds this way."

Then Beulah became embarrassed and put her head down. She was sorry she spoke. It sounded like a dumb idea.

Ranger Roger was silent. He was thinking.

"Hmmm," he muttered. "You know that just might work. Come on, get into my helicopter!" he ordered.

With long strides, Ranger Roger marched right up to his helicopter with Beulah hopping right alongside. He opened the door for her and she hopped in.

"Fasten your seat belt," he instructed as he sat down beside her.

Then he started the motor and the helicopter lifted right off the ground, higher and higher it went. Beulah could see all the Snow Bunnies still sitting and thinking. They will never believe her when she tells them she flew in Ranger Roger's helicopter.

Ranger Roger was flying right towards a great, white snow cloud. It was loaded with snow and it was headed towards Thunder Mountain. Ranger Roger came along side of the snow cloud and revved his giant propellers. Soon the snow cloud began to change direction.

"It's turning! It's turning!" shouted Beulah, excitedly.

Ranger Roger nodded and smiled. Soon the big snow cloud was right over Pine Mountain, right over the Snow Bunnies who were all looking up in surprise. And then the big snow cloud dropped all of its snow right on Pine Mountain, right on the Snow Bunnies.

Beulah could see all of the bunnies dancing and waving their arms. They were as happy as could be. Then Ranger Roger flew after an even bigger snow cloud and steered it right over Pine Mountain and it dropped all of its snow. Now there was tons of snow all over Pine Mountain.

Ranger Roger landed his helicopter right next to the Snow Bunnies who were playing and frolicking by now. He jumped from his pilot's seat and all the Snow bunnies hopped over to greet him, shouting, "Hooray for Ranger Roger! Thank you, Ranger Roger!"

"Oh, don't thank me," Ranger Roger said quietly.

The Snow Bunnies all became quiet. What did he mean, 'Don't thank me!'

"What do you mean?" asked Bernie Bunny. "We saw you fly your helicopter right up to the big snow cloud and push it right over Pine Mountain so it could drop all of its snow. And it did!"

"And we saw you fly over to that other big snow cloud and push it so it would drop all of its snow on Pine Mountain," exclaimed Bobbette Bunny, "And it did!"

"Yes, it did," added Billy Bunny.

"Yes, it did!" all the Snow Bunnies shouted. "We saw it!"

"But it wasn't my idea to push the snow clouds over Pine Mountain," Ranger Roger declared.

The Snow Bunnies were bewildered. They looked at each other, searching for an explanation.

"Well then, whose idea was it?" asked Burman Bunny.

Ranger Roger turned towards Beulah Bunny who was standing near the helicopter with her head lowered, rather shy.

"It was Beulah's idea."

"Beulah?" questioned Bertha Bunny.

"Yes, Beulah," repeated Ranger Roger.

All the Snow Bunnies stared at Beulah with their mouths open.

"She told me she tried to tell you but you wouldn't listen. Is that true?" asked Ranger Roger.

"I guess so," mumbled Barry Bunny, with his eyes cast downward.

"Don't you think you should at least have the courtesy to listen to someone before you reject what they have to say?" asked Ranger Roger.

The Snow Bunnies were all embarrassed. "Yes, sir," whispered Bobby Bunny.

"Well, why don't you all go over and thank Beulah for bringing you all of this snow."

The Snow Bunnies all lifted their heads and smiled at Beulah. Then all hopped over. "Thank you, Beulah," they shouted as they pushed and shoved to give her big hugs. Beulah was delighted at all of this show of affection.

"Will you build a snowman with me?" asked Barbie Bunny.

"Will you toboggan with me?" asked Benny Bunny.

"Oh, yes, I will play with all of you," cried Beulah. And they all hopped away to begin their play.

Ranger Roger smiled to see all of the Snow Bunnies having such a wonderful time. Then he flew his helicopter back to his cabin as all the Snow Bunnies waved good-bye.

Ranger Roger took a good look around before he turned and went into his cabin. Yes, he thought, this will be a good season for our tourists. Then he telephoned the manager of the Pine Log Lodge.

"Henry," he said in a serious voice, "there's plenty of snow on Pine Mountain!"

Manager Henry became so excited that he hung up the phone as soon as he thanked Ranger Roger for the good news. Then he shouted to all the employees that there was plenty of snow on Pine Mountain and that this would be a fine season for the tourists.

All the employees cheered and began to prepare the rooms for all the tourists who would be arriving soon.

"It would be a White Christmas after all," they cheered.

"And a Merry one," someone added.

THE END

MUSSO THE MOUSE

CHAPTER ONE

Once there lived a little mouse, Musso was his name. He had two cute little mousey ears and a very short tail. What? A mouse with a very short tail! How can this be, you ask. Well, this story will explain how Musso's tail became very short.

To begin, Musso lived with his mother, Mrs. Mouse, in a very cozy nest. Their front door came right out into the cozy kitchen of a cozy house in the little village of Nooseville. In the cozy house lived Mr. and Mrs. Bygolly and their children Ollie and Mollie. Ollie and Mollie were only ten and nine and after school and during vacation time they loved to play. When the weather was nice, they played outside. When it was snowing, raining or too cold, they played inside. But outside was more fun. They had many friends to play with which was also very much fun.

Ollie and Mollie had a puppy named Polly. She wasn't really a puppy since she was almost two years old but the children referred to her as their puppy. Polly was lots of fun and loved to play with Ollie and Mollie. Polly could fetch a ball or a stick or find Ollie and Mollie when they hid from her. Polly could always find Ollie and Mollie no matter where they hid. She knew their special scents and could follow them better than any old pedigreed hunting dog.

Sometimes Musso would peek out and see Ollie and Mollie and Polly running about. He wished he could join them. It looked like such fun.

"Not on your life!" warned Mrs. Mouse. "You can't go out and play with them. They will only want to catch you and put you in a trap. That's what they did to your poor father. Humans, dogs and cats don't want to play with mice!"

Musso could not understand but he knew he had to obey his mother. It made him sad to think that he could never play with the people in the house. He was sure those children and that dog would like him.

At night, Mrs. Mouse would creep out of her cozy nest and hunt for food. Musso had to stay where it was safe and wait for his mother to come home. He would wait impatiently, wondering what she would bring and get very excited when he heard her come through the front door. Sometimes she would have to sneak out two or three times in order to find enough for them to eat. And sometimes she would come running home as fast as she could with Polly chasing right behind her. Musso could not understand why Polly would want to chase his mother.

"When I grow up," Musso exclaimed, "I will give that dog a good scolding."

Then he would give his mother a hug and she would smile warmly at her sweet little son.

Mrs. Mouse usually brought bread crumbs or some cereal or some meal or some rice or bits of vegetables for Musso to eat. But his favorite was the food his mother called CHEESE!

"Uuuummmm!" Musso would cry out when his mother brought him a nice piece of cheese. He gobbled it right up without his mother's prompting. Sometimes she would have to prompt him to eat his cereal or vegetables.

Mrs. Mouse would frequently tell Musso that Mrs. Bygolly was a good housekeeper and swept up most of the food that spilled from the table or the stove.

"I wish Mrs. Bygolly wasn't such a good housekeeper," Musso would complain when he had to go to bed without any supper.

One night when Mrs. Mouse was fast asleep, Musso woke up. He was hungry. Maybe he could go into the cozy kitchen and find something good to eat. Maybe there was some of that cheese lying around. The more he thought about food, the bolder he became. So he quietly slipped out of his cozy bed and into the cozy kitchen.

My, what a big room this is, he thought, as he scurried behind the big black wood-burning stove where the good smells would come from at supper time.

"Oh, here are some crumbs," he exclaimed and he quickly ate them up.

"Boy, this is fun," said Musso, after he gobbled those crumbs.

He scurried out from behind the stove and saw a door that was partly ajar. He peeked in, sniffing all the time for food but he also sniffed for Polly. If he smelled her, he knew he had to run home or hide.

What he saw in the room were two little chests of drawers and two little beds. Ollie and Mollie must sleep in those beds, he thought. He was so intent on staring at the beds that he stopped sniffing. Suddenly he heard a "Grrrrr!" There was Polly, lying between the two little beds with her head raised. She must have smelled me, Musso thought.

He twirled around and dashed for home with Polly growling and barking close behind. Musso ran behind the big black stove. Polly slid into the stove with a BANG!, thrusting her muzzle under the stove while she barked.

The noise woke everyone. All the Bygollys hurried into the kitchen. Mrs. Bygolly lit the lamp and all watched Polly bark and growl.

"It must be a mouse," said Mr. Bygolly. "I will set the trap."

The lamp was put out and all went back to bed.

Musso raced through his front door and jumped into the cozy bed, snuggling against his mother who was wide awake. She nuzzled her frightened little boy.

"So, you went out of the cozy nest and disobeyed your mother?" she asked.

Musso nodded and pressed closer to her.

"You must wait until you are a little older. Then mother will show you how to explore the kitchen. Now they will set the trap," she continued. "If you see a big piece of cheese on the floor, do not try to eat it! The trap will get you. Do you understand?" she asked.

"Y-y-yes, mother," Musso whispered. What was a TRAP, he wondered.

Mrs. Mouse licked Musso's little ears until he fell into a deep sleep and dreamed about a very big piece of cheese.

CHAPTER TWO

In the morning, while Mrs. Mouse was still asleep, Musso peeked out of his cozy nest. He saw Mr. and Mrs. Bygolly go outside. Mrs. Bygolly often walked her husband to work in the morning since it was only a short distance away. Then she would come home and make breakfast for the children. Mr. Bygolly was a very good tinker.

"My goodness," Musso exclaimed.

Right near his front door, in the cozy kitchen, was the biggest piece of Swiss cheese he ever saw. Mrs. Bygolly must have missed that when she left with Mr. Bygolly, he thought.

Musso stuck his little head out the door and sniffed for Polly and the children. Mice are very good sniffers. But all he could smell was that wonderful Swiss cheese. Then he ventured further.

"Oh, oh," he whispered.

There was Polly, sleeping in the doorway of the children's room. She must be guarding them from mice, Musso thought. She is so far away, I could get that cheese and be safely home before she could get me, he speculated.

Poor Musso completely forgot his mother's warning about the trap. All he could think about was how surprised his mother would be when he brought her that big piece of cheese for breakfast.

Slowly he crept from the cozy nest into the cozy kitchen. Closer and closer he crept towards the cheese, stopping every few inches to sniff and look. But Musso did not see that Polly had one eye open and was watching the whole thing. She was waiting for Musso to get further away from his front door. Like all good hunters, Polly waited patiently for the best time to catch the prey.

Instinctively Polly knew that once Musso got to the cheese, he would become careless and easier to catch. It was a game of dog and mouse. Polly lay motionless, watching. Her body was tense, like a coiled spring, ready to leap forward and pounce on poor, unsuspecting Musso.

Musso was now at the cheese. He started to nibble. Suddenly, the cheese seemed to jump up. Musso was very fast and jumped back instantly. Then there was a loud "SNAP!" and Musso felt a terrible pain in his little tail. At that very moment, Polly sprang forward, snarling and barking.

Musso was so confused that he ran the wrong way and trapped himself in a corner, behind a chest. Mrs. Mouse jumped up when she heard all of the commotion and peeked out of her door. Her poor baby was cornered. She ran out, right past Polly's nose. Polly turned his attention to Mrs. Mouse and chased her back into her nest.

By now Ollie and Mollie were out of their beds and peeking around the chest where they first saw Polly barking. Ollie moved the chest a little and there was poor, frightened little Musso, shivering in the corner. Part of his tail had been snipped off by the trap.

"Awww," sighed Mollie. "The poor little mouse hurt its tail and is frightened."

She carefully picked up Musso and cradled him in the palm of her hand. Ollie peered at the little gray mouse. Polly came over and began to bark.

"Quiet! Sit!" Ollie commanded and Polly obeyed but she still wanted a better look at that mouse that she could smell.

"Here," Mollie said to Ollie and place Musso in his hand.

Ollie cupped his hands together and stared at Musso. Mollie made a tiny bandage and fixed it to Musso's tail. All the while Mrs. Mouse looked out anxiously. What were they doing to my baby, she wondered.

"There, little mouse," Mollie exclaimed. "Now you will be all better. Do you think his tail will grow back?" she asked her brother.

"Probably," Ollie answered with certainty.

"He was probably hungry and wanted that cheese," Mollie said.

"Yes," replied Ollie. "Let's give it to him."

"Oh, yes," exclaimed Mollie.

So she lifted the cheese from the trap and gave it to Musso who was still in Ollie's hands. Then Ollie placed Musso on the floor and ordered Polly to "Stay!" Polly wiggled a little and whined. She wanted to give that mouse a good chase!

"Stay!" repeated Ollie.

Musso ran for the cozy nest, the big piece of cheese held tightly in his mouth. Mrs. Mouse watched in disbelief. The humans gave her son cheese and let him go. She greeted her son enthusiastically and the two shared a delicious cheese breakfast. But Musso got a good scolding for disobeying his mother again.

No sooner had Musso disappeared into his nest when Mrs. Bygolly came through the door. She was a little surprised to see the children standing in the kitchen.

"The mouse got the cheese," Ollie explained and knew he just told a fib.

Polly whined a little. Mrs. Bygolly looked at the sprung trap and saw the cheese was indeed gone.

"Oh, well, I'll fix the trap after breakfast. Are you ready to eat?" she asked.

"Oh, yes," the children replied. Polly gave a bark which said she was ready, too.

"I shall make some pancakes with hot maple syrup," she announced.

"I can eat four," cried Ollie.

"I want four, also," said Mollie.

"And four you shall have, my dear children" said Mrs. Bygolly.

From then on, Ollie and Mollie gave little pieces of cheese and bread to Musso while Polly looked on, wagging her tail. Musso would even take bits of food right out of the children's hands. Then he would scurry home to share with his mother who always looked on in disbelief.

And Musso would say to his mother, "See, Mother, I told you the children and their dog would like me."

Mrs. Mouse would just smile and nod in disbelief.

CHAPTER THREE

It was three o'clock in the afternoon. Musso was peeking out of his door and he saw Ollie and Mollie in the kitchen. Mrs. Bygolly had gone to the store, leaving the children to themselves.

"It looks like rain," Mollie remarked.

"Yes. Let's go down to the creek," Ollie suggested. "We can build a dam and make a little lake when the rain comes."

"Oh, yes," answered Mollie excitedly. "That's fun. Shall we bring Polly?"

"No, she will get full of burrs and all muddy. Then mother will be upset with us for tracking up the floor."

"You are right," Mollie responded.

So they donned their yellow raincoats, rain hats and rubber boots and set out for the creek which was almost a mile away. Polly wasn't happy about being left behind and stood up on her hinds legs at the window, barking and whining. She didn't hear where they were going but she wanted to run outside anyway. Then she flopped in the doorway to the children's bedroom and took a nap.

Soon it started to rain, lightly at first and then harder and harder. Mrs. Bygolly got home just as it started to rain. She came bustling through the kitchen door, her umbrella in one hand and a shopping bag full of fruits and vegetables in the other. She called to the children. When they didn't answer, she looked at the pegs where their raincoats were hung and saw they weren't there.

They must have gone to visit one of their friends, she presumed. Then she began to prepare supper which would consist of a delicious vegetable soup, sourdough bread and fruit. She hummed quietly as she cleaned and chopped the vegetables. A large pot of water was already simmering on the stove.

The rain showed no signs of letting up and thunder and lightning were crashing and flashing frequently. Polly whined and shivered with fright in the corner. Musso snuggled against his mother. He didn't like all that scary noise.

Mrs. Bygolly kept looking out the window for the children. "I wish they would come," she said. "This is going to be a bad storm."

By now it was 5:00. She put on her raincoat, picked up her umbrella and Mr. Bygolly's raincoat and went to Mr. Bygolly's shop to make sure he didn't get soaked coming home. Polly wanted to come but Mrs. Bygolly made her stay in the house.

Pretty soon Mr. and Mrs. Bygolly hurried through the door. "Children," Mrs. Bygolly called. "Not home yet," she exclaimed. "Now I am angry. They know they must be home before 5:00."

"Maybe they are waiting for the rain to stop," Mr. Bygolly offered.

"They have their raincoats and hats," retorted Mrs. Bygolly, pointing to the empty pegs on the wall where their rain clothes were always hung. "I will go to the Mullers and you go to the Fritzes. Those are the only places they would visit. Come right back and we will meet here."

"Okay," replied Mr. Bygolly, a little reluctantly. But he could sense his wife was concerned so he agreed. The children will be at one place or the other, he was sure.

So they trudged out into the storm, each going a separate way. The storm was not easing. The creek will surely overflow, thought Mr. Bygolly. It always did when it rained this hard.

In less than ten minutes the two were back, one only a minute behind the other. Mr. Bygolly got home first without the children. Mrs. Mouse was beginning to worry for the children, too. It was a bad storm.

Then Mrs. Bygolly came home.

"Where are the children?" she asked, anxiously.

"They weren't there. You didn't find them either?"

"No," she answered. "Where can they be?"

Both stood helpless for a moment and just stared at each other.

When Mrs. Bygolly came home without the children, Musso scurried over to Polly.

"They said they were going to the creek," he whispered. "Do you know where that is?"

Polly barked affirmatively and stood up.

"Wait, I want to come with you," Musso called.

He quickly climbed up on Polly and nestled under her collar, clinging tightly to her soft fur.

Hmmm, Musso thought, Polly is as soft as my mother.

With Musso safely in place, Polly ran to the door and began to bark.

"Do you know where the children are?" asked Mr. Bygolly.

Polly barked several times and scratched at the door. Mrs. Bygolly looked on, anxious for any clue as to where the children might be. Mr. Bygolly opened the door and Polly ran out with Mr. and Mrs. Bygolly right behind. When they reached the edge of town, Mr. Bygolly told Mrs. Bygolly to get some of the neighbors and follow.

"I think they are at the creek," he shouted.

"The creek!" Mrs. Bygolly gasped. "Not the creek in this storm."

Now Mrs. Bygolly was very frightened and she hurried to the nearest house and banged on the door.

Mr. and Mrs. Carl were just sitting down to dinner. Mr. Carl opened the door.

"Quick, the children are lost by the creek! Follow my husband!" Mrs. Bygolly shouted.

Mr. Carl looked out and could barely see Mr. Bygolly running down the road. He grabbed his raincoat and ran after him. Mrs. Bygolly was already at the house next door. Soon ten men and their sons were running down the road towards the creek with Mrs. Bygolly right on their heels.

CHAPTER FOUR

Polly picked up the scent of Ollie and Mollie right away and followed it, running as fast as she could. Even this big rainstorm couldn't wash away the scent of the children.

Musso hung on tightly. He was very wet, just like Polly. Mr. Bygolly was getting further behind but by the time they reached the edge of town, he knew that Polly was headed for the creek. He knew he might need help and he could count on good friends and neighbors.

When Polly got to the creek, the banks were already overflowing and water was rushing past. Polly could not smell the children with this much water around so she ran up and down the bank of the creek, barking and looking all about.

Suddenly, Polly heard a faint call. Musso heard it, too.

"Polly! Polly!"

Polly looked about, trying to locate the sound but the noise of the rain, the rushing water and thunder confused her. She barked excitedly.

"Polly! Help!"

It was definitely Ollie and Mollie. But where were they?

"It sounded like over there," cried Musso, "to the left and across the creek."

Polly ran to the left, scanning the opposite bank. Then she heard Mr. Bygolly call.

"Polly, where are you?"

Polly barked loudly but kept looking for the children. Then she heard them call again. They were very close. Yes, there they were, on the other side, up in a big oak tree. Polly barked and barked. The children knew Polly could see them.

"Get father. Hurry!"

Polly stood at the edge of the water, barking. Mr. Bygolly finally caught up with her. Polly was looking right at the children. Mr. Bygolly saw them now. He shouted excitedly and waved.

Suddenly he realized that the tree which saved his children was getting ready to fall into the creek. The dirt around its roots was being washed away. If the children fell into that raging water they would perish. The tree was still upright for the moment but the roots were exposed and the water level was rising. The tree was beginning to tilt!

Now Mr. Carl arrived. Then the rest of the men and their sons and finally poor, frantic Mrs. Bygolly. One of the men brought a great length of strong rope. Mr. Bygolly grabbed it.

"If we can get the rope to the children, they can tie it around the tree trunk and slide across," he gasped.

"But who can cross such a river?" asked one of the men.

"I will try," replied Mr. Bygolly.

Polly barked loudly and put her front paws into the water. I can do it, she tried to tell them.

94

"Wait," said Mr. Carl. "Will the dog go to the children?"

"Yes," Mr. Bygolly quickly answered.

Tie one end of the rope around her collar and see if she can swim across. Then the children can reach down and tie the end to the trunk. If the dog can't make it, we can pull her back."

All agreed and one end of the rope was tied around Polly's collar.

"Go to Ollie and Mollie," Mr. Bygolly ordered.

Without hesitation, Polly leaped into the rushing water like an experienced Labrador. She paddled strongly against the rushing water as the rope was slowly let out by the men. Musso hung on tightly.

Ollie slid down the tree and stood at the base, one hand reaching for Polly and the other tight around the trunk.

Polly was almost there but all could see she was tiring.

"Come on, Polly," Ollie urged. "Come on!"

Finally, she was in reach of Ollie and he grasped her collar and pulled her out of the water. When Ollie grabbed hold of Polly, everyone cheered. Ollie was surprised to see little rain-drenched Musso under Polly's collar. Ollie picked up Musso and put him in the breast pocket of his shirt.

Mr. Bygolly shouted to his son, "Climb the tree and tie the rope around it tightly. Then you and Mollie slide across. We will catch you."

Ollie handed Polly to Mollie and then climbed as high as he dared. He tied the end of the rope around the trunk. Mollie made Polly sit on a large branch and climbed up to Ollie. Since the end of the rope was much higher than the other end across the river, the rope was like a slide. Mollie could just lock her ankles around the rope and use her hands to glide across. It was scary but she knew she had to do it. She started across. The rushing water below frightened her. It was like a trap, waiting to consume her.

When she was almost across, her ankles lost their grip and her legs swung down, leaving her dangling above the rushing water. She was hanging onto the rope with both hands but slowly losing her grip.

Everyone gasped. Mollie hung on tightly and began to swing the remaining few yards monkey-style. As soon as she was within reach, Mr. Bygolly grabbed her and pulled her to safety and into Mrs. Bygolly's waiting arms.

Now it was Ollie's turn.

"Come on," the men shouted. The tree began to creak and sway. The ground continued to give way. Ollie had Polly in his arms. How could he get across carrying her?

"Let the dog go," his father shouted. "Save yourself."

Ollie hesitated. How could he abandon poor Polly?

Suddenly the tree began to fall. It was too late. Ollie had one arm around Polly and the other around the trunk. Musso buried himself deeper in Ollie's pocket and closed his eyes.

Everyone screamed and ran to get out of the way of the falling tree. But the tree was so tall that when it fell, it actually spanned the overflowing creek. Some of the branches were so strong that the tree never fell into the water. The tree became a bridge with Ollie still hanging on, lying on its thick trunk.

Mr. Bygolly quickly climbed on the trunk and made his way to Ollie who still had one arm around Polly. Mr. Bygolly picked up Polly and helped his son walk across the tree to safety. Many eager arms were outstretched to help Mr. Bygolly and Ollie.

When all were safe, everyone marched home triumphantly for a job well done.

Mrs. Bygolly's soup was still simmering in the dying flames of her wood stove. The bread was done and still warm, well, warm enough.

As soon as everyone had on dry clothes, Mrs. Bygolly finished preparing supper.

Ollie set Musso on the floor and he ran to his mother. Ollie and Mollie dried Polly thoroughly and gave her a fine soup bone for supper.

Then the Bygollys sat at their table and Mr. Bygolly gave an extra prayer of thanks before everyone had their fill of hot, delicious vegetable soup, fairly warm sourdough bread with butter and apples and pears. Even Mrs. Mouse and Musso were rewarded with a very large piece of Swiss cheese which they ate right next to Polly.

Everyone lived happily ever after and all because a little mouse got his tail caught in a mouse trap.

THE END

POETRY

THE FOURTH OF JULY

Did you hear of Paul Revere
Who rode his horse that fateful year?
He warned us all to be alert
And then the war which made us free,
Began at dawn, at half-past three.
We won the war as all did see,
Because Paul rode so speedily!

MARY HAD A LITTLE LAMB

Mary had a little lamb,
She also had a ewe.
Once she gave a dinner
And put them in a stew!

THE OX AND THE FOX

In a stable lived an ox,
Also there was Benny Fox
Who made his den inside a box.

Benny Fox wore bright red sox
Which struck the fancy of the ox.
"Why do you wear those bright red sox?"
Asked the curious, big old ox.
"Why, to keep my feet warm," said the fox.

The ox and the fox in the stable lay
Until the fox just went away.
"Moooo! My friend the fox did stray,"
Cried the Ox as he munched his hay.

PIG OUT

The pig went to a restaurant
And read from the menu.
He looked for things to order,
Enough to fill up two!

Perhaps a slab of bacon
With a loaf of rye,
Yes, that will nicely do!

Bring some potatoes
And filet O' fish,
All of this was heaping
On too small a dish.

Let's try some other entrees
Just one of each for now
And while I am a-waiting,
A large side of cow.
For dessert? Oh, something light
Cookies, cakes and such
With a quart of ice cream,
That won't be too much.

With all this talk of eating,
His mouth began to froth
"One last thing," he said to the chef,
"Forget all your fine china,
Just bring me a trough."

A HOUSE OF LOVE

In this house let no voice rise,
And never shall an angry word
E'er be spoken, e'er be heard.

Words soft-spoken from the heart
Just for us to hear,
Will be whispered for your ear
From my heart for you to hear.

THE SPIDER AND THE ANT

Itsy-bitsy spider eating a loaf of bread,
Along came a little ant and this is what he said,
"If I get some jelly, may I have some bread?"
"Yes," said the spider, "Yes," the spider said.
"Thank you," said the ant and away he sped.

The ant returned with a jar of jam,
"Look at all this jam," he said,
"It will make a perfect spread!"
"Yes," the spider then replied
And to the bread the jam applied.

And so the two ate jam and bread
Until the loaf was through.
And when the sun began to set,
'Twas time to bid adieu.

Before they went their separate ways,
One to the other said,
"Let's meet again tomorrow
And share some jam and bread."

THE TOAD

The toad observed the traffic sign,
"NO PARKING HERE TODAY!"
The toad ignored the traffic sign,
Parked his car and went his way.
When the toad returned, to his dismay,
His car was not in place,
The car of toad was not in its space,
It seems it had been towed!

THE JUNGLE BAND

The boar could whistle through his snout
And make the weirdest sounds come out.
The elephant snorted through his trunk
And stomped his foot with
CLUNK! CLUNK! CLUNK!
The tapir tooted through his snoot -
A kind of rooty-toot-toot-toot!

So when you're in the jungle
And hear the lion's roar,
Listen to the noises
You've never heard before.

Hear whistles, snorts and toot-toot-toots
And then perhaps just one encore.
Oh, it will sound the mostest grand -
From the beasts out in the jungle land,
The beasts that joined the Jungle Band!

THE TEA PARTY

The wolf sipped from his cup of tea
And eye-balled each new attendee
Scones and cakes were not a treat,
What he craved was good red meat.

The rabbit, for a start would do,
Then perhaps a frog or two,
Followed by a beef fondue
And don't forget some mice, a few,
And finally, ere the day is through,
Roasted cat placed in a stew.

Yes, the wolf was always pleased
To come to parties, come to teas,
And say HELLO to all he'd meet
And see so many things to eat.

THREE PIGS AND THE WOLF

Can you guess what I just saw?
A pig who made a house of straw.
When the wolf blew with his might,
The house was blown clear out of sight.

His brother made a house of stick
It did not look so very thick
When the wolf gave it a kick,
Down it came, just that quick.

Another house was very slick
Built with neither straw nor stick.
This sturdy house was all of brick.
And when the wolf did blow and kick,
Nothing moved, not one lick.

Up the wall the wolf did scale
Then down the chimney he did sail
But below there was a pail
With boiling water. . . Did he wail!

The wolf does not approach this house,
The one made out of brick,
Three pigs reside with one pet mouse,
The wolf they did outslick!

VANITY

The rooster strode across the yard
Then perched atop the fence.
His chest he spread
As he cocked his head
To show his impor-tence.

Every morning was the same
Just at dawn, 'twas out he came
And took his place atop the fence
So all could see his own presence.

Every morning was a show,
He flapped his wings
And raised his head
And loudly he did crow.

COCK-A-DOODLE-DOO!

This cocky bird would have you know
That sun would rise when he did crow
And every day would remain dim
Without the crowing of the likes of him.

Anyone who heard
Had respect for this vain bird
Who pompously displayed contempt
For all of those whose heads were bent.

Then one morning,
Ere the dawn,
This rooster found
His voice was gone!

A cloth of wool
Was round his neck
To soothe his throat
Which was a wreck.

He made his strut across the yard,
Aware of every watchful eye,
Even with his scratchy throat
He would lift the sun up high!

He flapped his wings
And raised his head,
This silly pompous bird,
And then an awful screech was heard!

All observed and shrank in fear
The rooster's noise, for all to hear,
Was not the crow that raised the sun
And now what was there to become?

The rooster left his lofty throne
And crept back to his humble home
And all about began to wail
For surely now the day would fail!

But just as all were set to run,
Slowly rose the rising sun
And from that time the rooster's crow
Was nothing more than just a show.

For whether he would crow or not,
The sun would rise and be as hot
The crowing of that cocky bird
Was vanity to all who heard.

And no matter what you've heard
God's the one who makes a morn.
It's only vanity that makes a bird
Who thinks it's him who brings the dawn.

A THRIFT PLAN FOR THE ANIMALS

The woodman sat upon a log
With his knife and trusty dog
Then a moose came softly near,
Followed by an antlered-deer.

The moose sat down upon his rear
Then they all began a little chat
About the world and this and that,
Each made a point to hear.

The moose wished there would be more food
In winter months, you see.
The deer agreed and said more feed
Would ease the times severe.

"Maybe we could gather food
And store it for the cold?
And then our tummies would be full
With all that they could hold."

"Yes, let us gather while we can
Food to last the winter's span."
On this they all agreed
And listed what they'd need.

So they gathered extra food
While it was in abound
And stored it where it could be found
When snow was on the ground.

That winter all did eat their fill
Without a care of winter's chill.
So if you're wise you'll save today
And have some food for every day.

THE HYENA

The hyena lit a cigarette
And took a puff, a few.
Every day he smoked a pack,
Sometimes even two.

First he'd puff and then he blew
And then he'd give a giggle.
Was it the smoke that made him laugh?
No one really knew.

They all thought it was rather odd
To see him smoke and giggle
All would come to see him smoke
And watch his tummy wiggle.

The monkey took a little puff
To see if he would laugh
But he just coughed and fanned his tongue
And felt a pain right in his lung.

Then the zebra said he'd try
But smoke just rose and filled his eye
And tears began to show,
The smoke did make them flow.

Next the lion tried to smoke
But right away he gave a choke
He thought his throat had turned to rust
And spit the butt right in the dust.

If you don't want to cry and choke
Or act like a hyena,
Then make a promise to yourself
And never start to smoke!

THE EAGLE AND I

I soar with the eagle,
High in the sky,
Over treetops and mountains,
See how I fly.

My range has no limit,
My life has no bound.
When I'm far above the ground
I hear nothing, not one sound!

The eagle soars
Far from the rest
I called to him
And then I confessed,
To the Earth I'm confined,
To this Earth I am bind,

But nothing can stop me,
I fly in my mind.

GOODNIGHT

And now it's time to say goodnight
Our hour flew, it seems,
And now it's time to turn the light
And wish you happy dreams.
But I will think of you each day
Til it's story time again
But until then do something kind
And let a poem be on your mind!

I love you.

Mr. Ed

OTHER BOOKS PUBLISHED

YOU CAN ALWAYS TRUST YOUR AGENT - A humorous novel about a fourth-rate talent agent dealing with fifth-rate talent.

THE MIRACLE OF MICHAEL MURPHY - The story of a simple man who claims to have visions of Mary which unites people of all faiths throughout the world into prayer and creates a better world.

THE QUAGMIRE - This is a UFO adventure story about Bobby Hawks, a twelve-year-old boy who builds a Ham Radio set and comes in contact with aliens. The aliens prove to be hostile and he, his parents and his best friend must thwart the aliens who plan to conquer Earth!

SET OF THREE - $5.00

CHRISTMAS STORIES AND POEMS FOR CHILDREN - A collection of Christmas stories and poems.

WORK IN PROGRESS - WAR STORIES - A fictional account of events in WW II, Korea and Viet Nam.

DIRECT INQUIRIES TO: EZEDOK@JUNO.COM

Printed in the United States
200131BV00005B/265-504/A

9 781598 247053